ON BLACKBERRY HILL

Rachel Mann

on blackberry hill

RACHEL MANN

Praise for *On Blackberry Hill*

Mann weaves a poignant tale of loss and discovery that carefully builds to a hopeful, satisfying ending.
Wiley Blevins, author

Jewish summer camp is the perfect setting for a multi-generational novel: a daughter connects with her late mother through names etched in the bleachers, murals in the dining hall, and a mysterious stranger. Mann's compelling story and artful writing make this an excellent read for teens and adults.
Sarah Bunin Benor, winner, Sami Rohr Choice Award for Jewish Literature

Whether on the streets of New York or deep in the summer camp woods, Mann ensures the reader is as alive to every sight and sound as her central characters. Not only is the writing exquisite, but it had me in floods of tears by the end. I loved this book and so will you!
Justine Solomons, *Byte the Book*

For Bella, Ruby, and Louisa

1

Reena

Reena and her father were late for the Passover *seder*. "The only place in the country where there are enough Jews to jam the roads," her dad had said as they sat trapped on a bus in bumper-to-bumper traffic on the George Washington Bridge.

Fallwood, New Jersey was only about twenty miles from Manhattan, but it felt like a different planet: all those little pointy-topped houses laid out right next to each other, with tiny green front lawns broken up by driveways that touched the street like grey-blue streams. They walked from the bus stop on streets without sidewalks until they arrived at the Steins' own little stream.

The ceremony had already begun when they came in through the sliding back door. Her father put the macaroons he'd bought at Zabar's on the kitchen counter, and they tiptoed into the dining room and slid into the two empty seats at the table.

Reena's seat was next to Lila's, so there was no avoiding it: she'd have to talk to her cousin. Lila looked up at her and nodded silently, probably not wanting to interrupt the service. It was just as well, as they never seemed to have anything to say to each other.

When they were younger, the cousins had been mistaken for twins, with their brown curls and eyes, and round faces and freckles. But they were fourteen now, and those days were gone. Lila was wearing a dress with red flowers on it, her curls neatly arrayed beneath a headband with a matching flower. Reena had been to enough annual seders to know that her mother's family were a formal bunch, so she had worn her new purple jean skirt and a black sweater, and had pulled her wild curls into a ponytail. Her dad wasn't one for dressing up, though, and was wearing his normal attire: jeans and a wrinkled button-down.

Zeyde, their grandfather, was saying the *kiddush*, the blessing over the wine. Even though it was Mara and Gary's house, Zeyde sat at the head of the table and was in charge. With his greying beard and dark glasses, he had a rabbinical air to him, though he was a high school science teacher by profession. He loved his Jewish traditions, and he broke the middle matzah with fervor, carefully wrapping half of it in a blue paper napkin and placing it behind him on the mantel: the *afikoman*. Reena remembered this part; Zeyde was going to hide the *afikoman* and the kids would have to find it, though they weren't little anymore.

Next, eleven-year-old Nathan recited the Four Questions. Reena was grateful that he was the youngest, as she could never have sung anything in Hebrew. She picked up the *Haggadah* and read to herself in the English translation: "Why is this night different from all other nights?" The adults— Grandma and Zeyde, and Mara and Gary—sang in chorus: "*Ha-lila Ha-zeh, Ha-lila Ha-zeh kulo matzah . . .*" Her father glanced at her book to see what page they were on.

"Let's go around the table and hear about the Four Sons," Zeyde said. "*B'Ivrit*, in Hebrew, if you can, please! Lila, will you please tell us about the Wise Son?"

Lila read the paragraph in Hebrew without hesitation, her hoarse voice accentuating the guttural sounds of the language. Grandma nodded and smiled, enjoying the performance.

Zeyde asked Dad to read about the Wicked Son— on purpose, Reena wondered? Her father was made of something different from her mother's family—he never wore a tie like Uncle Gary, he never went to synagogue, and it was no secret that he didn't believe in God, at least not the god from the Exodus story.

Then Zeyde looked at Reena, over the top of his bifocals. She felt her face go red. She looked at her father, as if he might get her out of it, but he just tipped his head at her, encouraging her to start. She read the English quietly and quickly, eager for it to be over. The passage was the one about the Son Who Does Not Know How to Ask.

The *seder* went on. Reena found the readings mysterious. She had endless questions. It wasn't that she didn't know how to ask, but rather, whom would she ask? Her father couldn't help her. He knew no more than she did about the passage that read: "And the Lord brought us forth from Egypt. Not by a ministering angel, not by a fiery angel, not by a messenger angel, but by Himself."

Her mother had believed in angels. She knew this because her father had shown her a series of portraits that she had done of regular people in old-fashioned clothes, with amused and joyous expressions on their faces. At the bottom of each drawing she'd written the word "Angel." If only her mother were there to help her understand.

Reena had forgotten how long it takes to get to the meal. She was tired of readings in a mysterious foreign language and her stomach was growling. Her father was clearly thinking the same; he was shaking his left leg the whole time, making it even harder for her to wait. Finally he stood up. She heard the bang of the metal screen door off the kitchen, and she knew he was having a cigarette. Grandma whispered something in Aunt Mara's ear.

As Aunt Mara began reading about the plagues, Lila pushed her chair back, stretched, and mumbled louder than she needed to, "bathroom break."

Reena knew that Lila was scheming to grab the *afikoman*. It was the same every year, and she'd long given up caring. She got up, anyway, to stretch her legs, and went into the living room. Lila wasn't there.

Reena looked at the dark wood bookcase full of books and photos in frames. She was drawn to a shiny metal frame that held a small photo of her and Lila as babies, crawling on the floor. Baby Lila was distracted by a toy, but the baby version of herself stared straight at the camera with wide, searching eyes. She wondered if it was taken before or after her mother died.

Behind the photo was a box of yellowing letters and ancient glossy photographs. She picked out a letter addressed to Mara, and put it back, feeling she probably shouldn't go through her aunt's personal things. But she was curious, so she flipped through some of the photos. There was one of Aunt Mara and her mother in one-piece bathing suits, with a lake behind them. And there was one of Mara laughing with a guy with shoulder-length straight hair—it took her a moment to realize it was her dad. Lean, square-jawed, and with all that hair; he was so young! Then she found one of her mother wearing a short skirt, looking directly at the camera with wide eyes. Reena wondered what she might have been thinking at that moment. Behind her mother, half turned away, stood a skinny guy with a straggly beard.

"Whatcha doing?" Lila said, sneaking up on her from behind.

"Nothing. Just looking."

"Let me see," Lila said.

She held the last photo out to Lila. "Who's that?" Reena asked.

"What do you mean? It's Naomi. Your mom. Duh. These must be my mom's old camp pictures."

"I know that. I meant—" Reena felt stupid for asking. Lila wouldn't know who the guy in the background was; she hadn't been there, after all.

"So what should I do with the *afikoman* ?" Lila asked, holding the special matzah up triumphantly. "Zeyde's pathetic at hiding it. I saw him put it under a chair. Now *we* just have to hide it so that we'll know where it is but he won't!"

"Maybe under the couch?" Reena asked, slipping the three photographs in the pocket of her jean skirt. She didn't think Mara would miss them, lost in an old box, and she wanted to look at them again.

"No. He'll look there first. And last year we put it in the dryer so he already knows to look there, too."

"What about behind the computer screen?"

"No, too obvious," Lila said.

Reena looked around the living room, trying to be helpful.

She saw a black rectangular machine above the DVD player, with a hole like a mail slot, just the perfect size to fit half a piece of matzah.

Aunt Mara called, "Kids, back to the table!"

"I know!" Reena whispered, pointing to the spot. Lila panicked and passed the *afikoman* to her like a hot potato. She shoved it in, feeling the fragile cracker break as it crunched into the slot. They dashed back to the table. There wasn't any rule about the *afikoman* having to be unbroken, was there?

"Time for the Hillel sandwich," Zeyde was saying.

He handed everyone a matzah sandwich, which for the kids was filled with *haroset*, an apple, nut and sweet wine mixture. Adults Zeyde liked got half *haroset* and half *maror*, or bitter herbs.

Zeyde handed her father a sandwich filled only with *maror*—white horseradish.

Zeyde recited the blessings and everyone crunched into the matzah. Dad's face went bright red and he started dry choking. He grabbed the only glass in front of him, filled with sweet red kosher wine, and downed it. It was not his first glass of the night.

It was finally time to eat. Mara brought dish after dish of food: chopped liver, roast chicken, broccoli with almonds, *farfel kugel*, potato *kugel*.

Everyone ate hungrily and quickly, probably because they'd all been sitting at the dining table not eating for more than an hour. Also, the food was good: salty and rich. Her father ate quietly, taking big gulps of wine between bites. When his glass was empty, he looked around for the bottle. It was on the sideboard behind Aunt Mara.

"Could you please pass the wine?" he said.

Aunt Mara was talking to Grandma, and pretended not to hear. He asked again, and still received no answer.

So he stood up, and in the booming voice that he reserved for special occasions, like announcing the members of his jazz group, or getting Reena's attention in a crowd, he said, "COULD YOU PLEASE PASS THE WINE?!"

The table went quiet, and Mara looked up at him. "I think you've had enough, Jim," she said.

"Get off it, Mara," he said, quieter but still firm. Reena felt her cheeks turn the color of the wine. Gary rose and retrieved the bottle, and filled her father's glass. He also filled his own. Mara stood up, looking upset, and started to clear the plates away.

Reena heard Aunt Mara talking to Gary in the kitchen as she scraped and rinsed dishes. She could have sworn she heard her name mentioned. But why would they be talking about her? It was time for the *afikoman*.

"This year you will have to look for it," Lila told Zeyde, giggling. "You'll never find it!" She looked really proud of herself, and Reena felt a little annoyed that she wasn't giving her any credit. They'd hidden it together, after all. "Alright, then. Let's go have a look," Zeyde said. They guided him around the house using "hot" and "cold" hints. The whole family was in the den as Zeyde looked between the books on the shelves, inside the record player, and under the sofa cushions. Reena stood against a wall and watched, her heart beating fast. Then she saw Gary spot it—a tiny corner of blue napkin sticking out of the rectangular black box.

"What . . . the . . . HELL . . .?" he said under his breath as he dashed across the room. He opened the slot with his fingers and pulled out a scrap of blue paper. He tried again, and the matzah crunched in his fingers. He managed to pull out only a corner of cracker, and another piece of ripped napkin. The *afikoman* was stuck.

Gary spun around and glared at Lila. "You broke the VCR! Now how am I going to finish converting all the old home videos to digital? What the hell were you thinking putting a piece of matzah in the VCR?" He seemed to have forgotten that Reena was there. Reena wanted to disappear, or shrink down to Thumbelina's size and tiptoe away between everyone's giant shoes.

"But it was Reena!" Lila said, pointing at her nose. She stamped her foot and folded her hands across her chest. "She's the one who did it!" Reena couldn't believe it. It was Lila's crazy idea to hide the thing in the first place. Gary looked at Reena, shaking his head back and forth. Reena's father came to her side. "Now wait a second, let's not go accusing Reena of anything. The kids were together." Thank God for her dad. Any feelings of jealousy that she might have felt that night—about her cousins' big house, or their mom's cooking, or the way they could show off reading Hebrew in front of Grandma and Zeyde— were instantly forgotten. They didn't have her dad. Lila wasn't finished.

"But Reena put it there. I saw her."

"Reena?" Aunt Mara said, looking at her with raised eyebrows.

"I didn't know!" she said, and it was true. What was a VCR anyway?

Gary had nothing else to say. He sat down and desperately pulled broken pieces of matzah and little tufts of blue napkin from the mouth of the machine.

"You should teach your daughter a thing or two about behaving in other people's houses," Aunt Mara spat out at her father as she brushed past him.

Reena and her father didn't stay for the second half of the *seder*. On the bus home he explained all about videocassette recorders. He also mentioned he'd seen Mara toss the macaroons he'd brought in the trash. Apparently, they weren't kosher for Passover.

2

Naomi

(Twenty years earlier)

The morning after the seder, Naomi sat with her older sister Mara at the round table in the kitchen of their childhood home. Running her fingers over the checkered tablecloth that their mother only ever used during Passover, Naomi thought how new and strange it was to think of this place as her 'childhood home'. But now that she'd been at NYU for almost a year, that was how it felt. She knew she'd never move back in with her parents; that was for sure.

"I'm going to stay in the city this summer," Naomi said, taking a sip of tea out of a glass Passover mug.

"You're doing what?" her mother spat out, spinning around at the sink, where she was washing breakfast dishes.

"My friend Liz is, too. We're going to find a sublet and get jobs waitressing or babysitting." She cupped both hands tighter around the mug, as if it might give her strength. She knew her parents wouldn't like the idea of her staying in the city for the summer, and she was bracing herself for a fight.

"But the city is even more horrendous in the summer," her mother said, walking away from the sink, rubber gloves still on. "Have you ever been there when the streets seem like they might melt? I don't think you'll like it." She waved a dishtowel.

Here we go, Naomi thought. "I'm not worried about the heat, Mother. It's not like it's cool here on Long Island in the summer."

"I don't know, honey. We need to discuss this with your father."

After their mother left the kitchen to get ready for *shul*, Mara said, "What about camp? I thought you were going to be on waterfront again with Jennifer."

"I've barely spoken to Jennifer this whole year," Naomi said. "For all I know she's got some other exciting plan, too. And besides, I don't want to go to camp. My life is in the city."

"I think you're making a big mistake, not that you care what I think."

"You're the one who said it." Mara was less than two years older than Naomi, but she always acted like she had the wisdom of age and experience. It got on Naomi's nerves. Mara didn't understand her; none of them did. There were things happening in the city that they couldn't fathom—chance encounters with interesting people, the opportunity to be surprised.

—

Just a few days earlier she'd been sitting between classes on a bench in Washington Square Park. Sitting on a bench reading *Anna Karenina*, she felt the sun on her face, and heard the beat of a drum mixed with the rumble of buses. As she daydreamed, a guy came over to her, humming a tune.

"Are there blessings in your book?" he asked.

"Excuse me?" she said.

He was thin, with a long, blond beard, a tweed cap, and bare feet. He looked about her age.

"Do you sit in the sun on this day reading words in praise of God?"

Naomi wasn't sure if she should answer. She found it was better not to engage the Village deadbeats. But she didn't feel threatened; this one had a gentleness about him.

"It's nothing," she said, putting the book behind her.

"Praise Hashem," he said. "You shall discover the beauty of God's creation."

Naomi realized she'd made a mistake: he wasn't a local street kid, at least not a typical one. Maybe he was one of those cultish Jews out to convert the unreligious? She looked down at her lap. She felt even more awkward around certain Jews than she did around homeless vagrants. Despite what she considered a fairly religious upbringing, she suspected most of the Brooklyn black hats would hardly consider her a Jew.

She looked up and found him staring at her with unblinking, sparkling blue eyes. She noticed the clean line of his jaw, and his open expression. She was surprised how lovely he was to look at. So many of the guys she knew were aloof, anxious, or cynical. This one looked happy.

"Do not despair. Though you are lost, God will show you the way."

"I'm not lost," she said, reaching for her patchwork quilt bag. She didn't like the way he threw around the G-word as if he owned it. But though she'd intended to get up and walk away, she stayed put. She had an inexplicable feeling that she was meant to listen to him.

"I come with a message," he said, as if reading her mind.

"You do?"

"Follow the path of your heart to discover God's truth." He looked her in the eye again.

"The path of my heart?"

"The path to find love."

Naomi felt the hairs on her arms stand on end. What did it mean? She wasn't looking for love. Enlightenment, maybe. Excitement, definitely. Love, no. That was Mara's mission, not hers.

His head bowed, he backed away.

"But— " He turned and walked away before her lips could form the question. One minute she could see him walking through the throngs of people, slowly placing one foot in front of the other, and the next minute he was gone. She couldn't even figure out which direction he'd disappeared to. She sat still on the bench, thinking. He hadn't invited her to pray, to eat, or to learn: maybe he wasn't trying to convert her, after all.

She didn't know what it meant—meeting this oddball. But she loved that it had happened. Things like that don't happen in a place as ordinary as summer camp, Naomi felt certain.

—

That evening, as she was packing her things to return to the city—Naomi had classes the next day—her father came into her room.

"Your mother tells me you have some *farkakte* plan to stay in the city this summer?"

"Yes, Daddy. My friend Liz and I . . ."

He cut her off. "No, you're not. The city is no place for a girl on her own. It's one thing for us to send you there for an education, but that happens during the year, not in the summer. You think you're all grown up, but you're barely nineteen. You've still got some growing to do."

"But Daddy!" Naomi searched her father's eyes for some kind of understanding. They used to have that between them. She'd spent hours as a child in Daddy's little woodworking shop in the basement, watching him carve figurines and toy cars with his magical fingers, until the day when he'd finally handed her a knife and let her try. She thought she'd already earned his trust.

"What makes you think that your mother and I should support your summer of fun in New York City? You have real *chutzpah*."

"I'm not asking for your money, Daddy. I'm going

to get a job, and I can take care of myself. I'm going to stay in the city, because that's where I want to be. And that's that!" She had never raised her voice to her father before; her heart was racing.

"No, young lady, that is not that!" he boomed in her face and then stormed off, leaving her crying in a heap on the bedroom floor, surrounded by her old dolls.

In the evening, her mother drove her to the train station. They were silent the whole way, and parted with a wordless exchange of pecks on the cheek. Naomi hadn't said goodbye to her father.

—

A few days later, Naomi arrived back in her dorm room as the phone was ringing.

"Where have you been? I've tried you six times today," Mara said. She sounded exasperated, and possibly like she'd been crying.

"I was in class. What's wrong?"

"It's Mom and Dad. They are really upset with you."

"I know that," Naomi said. "But what's happened? Why are you crying?"

Mara sucked up her sniffles. "Dad is so worked up that he won't even speak to you. Mom begged me to call you and ask you to act sensibly."

"I *am* acting sensibly, Mara. It's our crazy parents that are going over the edge!"

"This isn't a joke. Dad said he'll stop paying your tuition if you disobey him. I tried to get him to back down, I really did. I've never heard him like this. Please come around—there will always be other summers. Please."

Naomi put her hand on her chest to try to slow the beating of her heart. She couldn't believe this was happening. Her parents didn't even have the courage to call her—they had called Mara! They used to do the same thing when she was a girl—enlist Mara's help to "talk sense" to her—as if she was some stubborn and irrational creature whom only Mara knew how to defuse. But Naomi didn't look up to her sister now the way she used to. Mara knew it, too. Naomi could tell by the way she was saying, "Please, Naomi, please," over and over.

Still, Mara's message dealt a heavy blow. Naomi couldn't continue at NYU without money for tuition. And where would that leave her? Moving back in with her parents. She thought of how impressed her art history professor had been by the paper she'd written on Manet. She could picture herself working in a museum, giving tours, teaching others to see in art all the things she saw. She had to return to college in the fall. Nothing else was as important.

"All right, I hear you," Naomi said. "I'll call them. Ok?"

"What will you say?"

"Would you like to tell me what to say, too?"

"No, no."

"I'll call them," Naomi said. "I've got to go now. Bye."

3

Reena

On one of the final afternoons of eighth grade, Reena came home from school and heard rustling in the bedroom. Her body tensed, her back still against the door. Ever since her father had made her a set of keys in fifth grade, she'd wondered what she would do if there was an intruder. There had been break-ins in her building; she knew it could happen. Scream and run, she figured.

She was fumbling in her bag for her cell phone, just in case, when her father walked out of the bedroom, whistling.

"What are you doing home at three pm?" she demanded. "You scared me half to death."

"I'm here to see you, Reen. How was your day?"

"Fine." She dropped her bag and looked at him. His eyes were smiling and she could tell he was really excited about something. A few things crossed her mind: he got a raise; he got a date; he won the lottery?

"Bob asked me to go on tour with him this summer, to Japan."

"Japan!" She gave him a hug. "That's amazing! I've always wanted to go to Japan. Can we go see Sumo wrestling? And take origami lessons from a master? Will we get to eat sushi every day?"

He pulled away from her. "Not you, honey. Me."

"What do you mean? Since when do you go anywhere without me?"

He was kneeling now, and holding her shoulders with his hands. "Reen, this tour is huge. When we come back there's going to be an album."

Her face went hot. She felt the closeness of tears, but she didn't want to cry.

"But what about me?"

"I'm really sorry, darling. This is no family tour. It's expensive, and I'm going to be super busy, and the hours will be really late and you just . . . can't. But it's okay. Mara's arranged for you to spend the summer with Lila and Nathan at Camp Tova."

"No!" she screamed, the anger tightening in her throat. It was one thing for him to leave, but it was another for him to send her away. "I will hate it there."

"You don't know that."

It was true, she didn't know for sure. But she knew enough about her cousins' camp to make a good guess. She knew that it was in the middle of nowhere, where there was no movie theater and no galleries and no all-night deli. She knew that it was religious; it was probably like a Jewish monastery for kids. She knew that none of her friends would be there. And, worst of all, she knew she'd be stuck with Lila, her frosty cousin.

She gripped a metal-framed dining chair with blanching fingers as her brain spun. "Maybe I could just stay here. You could ask Harold to check on me, make sure I'm taking out the garbage and washing the dishes. Or I'll move in with Alisa. I don't think her mom would mind. Or . . ."

Her father pulled her close, wrapping her in his long arms.

"I'm sorry, honey. This is just something that I have to do. You'll like camp. I didn't think I'd like it either and look what happened to me. If it weren't for that camp, I wouldn't have you."

It was no use. She pushed him away and ran into the bedroom, slamming the door. Why couldn't he see that she was too old for a hug to be a solution?

—

Sitting on a New Jersey Transit bus flying over the George Washington Bridge, Reena stuck her nose to the glass and stared back downtown at the giant, familiar buildings, their tops lost in the summer haze. The heavy heat of summer had already arrived. The air conditioning poured from the vents by the windows and she pulled her face away, protecting herself from the chill.

For some reason she thought it would be more bearable on the other side of the Hudson; but, when she got off the bus, she found the weather in New Jersey equally sticky.

"Oh, Reena, it's so good to see you," Aunt Mara said in one breath as Reena climbed into her car at the bus stop. Reena leaned in to let Mara give her a kiss. Instead of putting the car in drive, Mara let her eyes hang on Reena, taking her in as if it were some kind of miracle that she'd made it to New Jersey. It wasn't the first time Reena had noticed her aunt staring at her. Then, all at once, Mara sat up and drove away.

"Can you believe this?" she said. "Still only June and it feels like August. Looks like it's going to be a brutal summer."

Reena thought of her father, and the way he'd taken off without her. Yeah, brutal.

Her dad had said he didn't think he'd like camp. Considering how little Judaism he practiced—almost none, save for holidays at Grandma and Zeyde's—it was amazing he'd ever spent time in any Jewish camp. But he'd definitely been there, and survived. She hoped she would, too.

"Lila! Come say hi to Reena!" Aunt Mara yelled as they stepped through the back door into the kitchen. At first the house seemed completely empty, but then Reena heard scuffling coming from somewhere.

Nathan ran into the kitchen, panting as if he was being chased, but when he saw Reena he stopped on a dime. He opened the fridge door and stood there cooling himself.

"Hey, Reena," he said.

"Hey."

Nathan was always carrying a sketchbook and pencils—a pint-sized Matisse. Everyone said he took after his aunt Naomi—Reena's mother.

"Where's Lila?" Aunt Mara asked, adding before he could answer, "We're leaving soon. Make sure you're ready."

"I *am* ready! And Lila's in her room."

Reena found Lila sitting on her lavender carpet, texting. Reena wondered how she got her long curls to lie softly and neatly in a cascade down her back when her own seemed to do nothing but frizz and puff. Lila wiped a bead of sweat off her forehead with the back of her hand, laughing at something on her phone. Reena was afraid to interrupt her. She wanted to start things off on the right foot, as her dad would say.

Lila looked up. "Did you get the email?" she asked. "What cabin are you in? I'm in G-8."

"I didn't get anything."

"Must be because you signed up so late. I'm so excited because Becky and Allie and Janet and Michael are all in my cabin! Again! For the third year! It's so cool." She slipped her phone into a pink backpack.

"Michael?"

Lila pointed at her desk to a framed photo of a group of girls standing with their arms over each other's shoulders; she was in the center. "Michael's the one on the end. Red hair. I think they named her after a dead uncle or something."

Reena stared at the photo. The girls wore tight tanks and short shorts. They had smooth complexions and hair, their heads identically tilted to the side. She scanned their faces for signs of their personalities, but couldn't tell much. They looked too perfect, like an expensive package of genetically modified strawberries.

Lila looked up when she didn't respond. "Oh, sorry," she said.

"About what?"

"Um, just mentioning Michael's uncle. No offense."

"Not offended."

"Do you think about her?"

"My mother? I didn't even really know her so there's not much to think about."

"My mom's told me some things about her. You know, your parents met at Camp Tova."

"Yeah, I know."

Lila smiled, her eyes squinting. "Mom also told me that Aunt Naomi was very busy that summer she met your dad—flirting with just about every guy in camp. There was one other guy in particular she spent a lot of time with, so it was kind of a surprise that she ended up with your dad."

"Really?" Reena felt her mouth falling open, and made herself close it. This story was the last thing she expected to hear. She was kind of shy around boys— she didn't even know how to flirt—and she'd always imagined her mother had been like her. And that she'd loved her dad, only.

Lila shoved a bunch of magazines in her backpack. "Just think. If she had gone for the other guy, you wouldn't even be here."

"Time to go! Everyone in the car," shouted Aunt Mara from downstairs.

Lila grabbed her backpack and ran down the stairs. Reena had no choice but to follow her.

—

The ride felt long, but finally the car exited the highway and they were winding along small country roads with old red barns in the distance and cows by the side of the road. Mara's car followed a line of vehicles slowly nearing the mysterious destination in the woods. Soon they came to a green metal fence with a sign that said, "Welcome to Camp Tova." Nathan was squirming in his seat. It was hard to tell if he was excited or scared.

Counselors in red camp shirts with "STAFF" written on the back approached each car and helped the campers out, looking at their clipboards to tell them where to go. An older teenage boy told Nathan to follow him. Nathan kissed his mother and Reena saw that he was a bit teary.

"Come on, sweetie, you're going to have a great time," Mara said. "Visiting day is only in four weeks." Nathan held it together and followed his counselor.

A tall skinny counselor informed Reena that she was in cabin G-8, with Lila. "Do you girls know how to get there?" she asked.

"Of course I do," Lila said.

Lila kissed her mom goodbye, and started walking away. Reena turned to follow her, but Mara grabbed her hand, and looked at her with wide eyes—another of her intense stares. "You'll be okay," she said. Then she returned to the comfort of her air-conditioned car and drove down the dirt road that led out of camp.

4

Naomi

When the semester ended in May, Naomi returned home to live with her parents in Rosebury for the month before camp would begin. She moved back into her old bedroom, and found her bed felt too small, her feet always touching the wooden footboard. Still, she spent a lot of time there, reading until late at night and sleeping until noon. One day, a week after she arrived, her eyes opened on the pastel still life of oranges and apples that she'd made in ninth grade. The picture was flat and ordinary, and would have likely been thrown away with a pile of others if her mother hadn't had it framed. "Such talent," her mother had said, holding the picture up to admire it. Naomi knew, now, that she wasn't actually talented, in the destined-to-be-collected-by-rock-stars kind of way. Yet she still liked to draw, in secret, without the threat of criticism.

"So sleeping beauty rises," her mother said as Naomi came into the kitchen in her pajamas.

"G'morning, Mom," Naomi said.

"Morning! Hardly," she replied. "Would you like some coffee?"

"Yes, please." Naomi sat down across from Mara, who was reading the paper at the table. "What are you doing today?"

"Shopping with Mom. We're leaving in a few minutes. Do you want to come?"

"No, think I'll stay here."

"Naomi, come with us, sweet pea," her mother said, putting a hand on her back. "You've barely left the house since you got here last week. What are you going to do all day?"

"Um, might take a bath, or finish my book."

"All right, but I don't want you moping around all day in your pajamas. Please get dressed. And think about calling some of your friends from high school? I'm sure Beth would like to hear from you."

"Beth could just as easily call me."

"Naomi, my dear, when did you become such a grump?" her mother said, as she put her keys into her purse. "Chin up, it's a lovely day. At least go sit in the sun for a while in the backyard. It'll do you good. You've become positively nocturnal!"

Naomi rolled her eyes, but once she was alone in the house, she took her mother's advice. She found an old sketchbook and Cray-Pas in a drawer by the television, and perched herself on one of the white metal garden chairs. Drawing took all of her thoughts away; she felt calmer, even, than when she was asleep, when her mind was full of dreams and plans.

—

On Friday evening the family ate together in the dining room. The comfort of roast chicken and sweet noodle *kugel* made Naomi feel better than she had all week. "Mom, you need to write down some of your recipes for me," she said. "I never eat this well when I'm away at school."

"You just need to spend some time in the kitchen with me."

"Me, too. You said you'd teach me how to make chocolate mousse," Mara said.

"Of course, I'll teach both of you."

"Now, I don't want to take you from your cooking lessons, lucky as you two are to have the world's best to learn from," their father said, pointing his fork at their mother.

"Hush," their mother said, smiling.

"But I could use some help down in the shop,"

he continued. "I've just bought the wood to make a dresser."

"With drawers?" Naomi asked.

"Yes, indeed," he said.

"I'll help," Naomi said, thinking she could use a project.

"Good. I'll try to get out of the office early this week."

The table was quiet for a minute as everyone chewed and sipped.

"Now tell me," their mother said, "any special boys this year at school?"

Leave it to her to take advantage of a lull in conversation. Naomi shook her head and put a forkful of *kugel* in her mouth. No way she was going to talk about her love life at Shabbat dinner.

"No one, Naomi?" her mother pressed.

Mara gave Naomi a searing look, as if to say, don't lie. It wasn't really a lie; there hadn't been anyone special. There had been a few dates—if you can call coffee in a MacDougal café a date—with guys she'd met in classes. And there had been Johnny, a boy she met at a fraternity party who had planted a slobbery kiss on her mouth at the end of the night. But there had been nobody to tell her parents about.

"What about you, Mara? You don't mind sharing just a little. How are the Brandeis boys?"

"Nancy, leave the girls alone," their father said.

"It's alright," Mara said. "I can tell you. I went out a couple times with someone named Ted, but let's just say he wasn't for me. He's from Maine and wants to be a large animal vet." Their mother nodded, and Naomi tried to swallow a snort.

"What?" Mara glared at her sister. "And then there was this guy named Gary. He's from New Jersey, and he seems nice, but I'm not sure about him yet. Anyway, we're not like, a couple, or anything."

"Gary what?" their mother asked. "What town is he from? Maybe I know his parents."

"Stein, and he's from one of the Oranges, I think." Their mother shook her head, not able to place the family.

"What's this young man studying?" their father asked.

"He's studying math, Daddy. I don't know what he's planning to do after college, maybe teach." Mara pushed her food around her plate.

"Hmmm," their mother said. "Can you go to med school with a math degree? Or maybe do something with computers?"

"Stop it, Mom. "

Naomi couldn't believe that Mara was putting up with being grilled about a guy with whom she'd only been on a couple of dates.

"I'm not trying to rush you, sweetie," their mother said. "You girls should take all the time you need, being young, meeting people. You'll know when you find the one, just like I knew when I met your father."

Naomi thought her mother was putting on an act. All their lives they'd been hearing the story of their parents' glorious romance, ignited at a college dance in an era when colleges had dances. Mara only had one more year to find 'the one', as she was going to be a senior. And what was college for, according to their parents, if not to find a spouse?

Naomi had seen some of her classmates get so carried away with drinking and dating that they'd done badly on exams. What a waste: all those college kids squandering their brains and futures because of their base needs for sex and love. *Not me*, she thought. *I'll swear off men, if I have to, as hard as that may be. I want something more.*

—

"Please, Mara, keep an eye on your sister this summer," Naomi overheard late one morning, a few days before she and Mara were going to leave for camp. She stood still outside her parents' room, listening. Mara and their mother were sitting on the bed folding laundry.

"What do you mean?" Mara said. "She can obviously take care of herself."

"Yes, but that's not what I mean. There's something . . . something brewing in her. She'll barely talk to me. Haven't you noticed?"

"She's ok," Mara said. "She's probably still disappointed about the argument—you know she hates it when she doesn't get her own way. She told me she misses the city."

"I'm just glad she's going to camp, and that you two will be together."

Naomi entered the room then, stepping loudly to cut off their conversation.

"Give us a hand here, honey," their mother said, pushing the basket toward her.

Naomi sat down on the bed with them and folded one of her father's undershirts. Mara was right—she was bitter. Her friend Liz didn't have parents like hers—she'd found a summer job as a research assistant, and was renting a room on Thompson Street. But Naomi's parents had blackmailed her. Once they nixed her city plan, she'd been left with no choice, really, but to return to camp—she hadn't spent the summer at home since she was seven, and now that she was nineteen it was no time to start. Though she'd enjoyed her summers in camp as a child, the best she could hope for now was a repeat, a do-over, when what she wanted was a new adventure.

Her parents had proven they could control her life, but still her mother wanted more. Naomi grabbed another shirt but then, changing her mind, threw it back in the basket and retreated to her room.

A month later, Naomi stood at the mirror in the bathroom of cabin G-4, where she had been assigned to sleep for the summer. All of the waterfront staff "lived-in" with campers—in a few days' time, the cabin would be full of chattering, arguing, giggling twelve-year-olds. But just then it was quiet, as it was only the second day of Staff Week, and the two other counselors from her cabin were out at meetings.

Inspecting her face, she noticed she was already turning deep olive after only three days in the sun. When she was tanned she was sometimes mistaken for Italian—and even, once, Indian. She tied her long dark curls at the nape of her neck with a rubber band, and splashed water onto her cheeks and forehead. Then she glared into her own brown eyes as she thought about the strange guy she'd met that day in Washington Square Park.

The odd encounter had stuck with her. She hadn't even wanted to come back to camp—coming back had nothing to do with "following her heart." Not that she was looking for love, anyway. Because she wasn't. She grimaced. How absurd to let that oddball get under her skin. It was pathetic, really.

But the thing was, Naomi believed in fate, and that things happened for a reason. When she was younger she paid close attention to the weather on test days—rain almost always meant she'd do well. She would turn on the radio believing that if the next song broadcast was a love song, the boy she had her eye on would notice her. Though she was no longer the girl who used to walk all the way home from school without touching a crack in the sidewalk, Naomi held on to her belief in the world's magic and mystery. That strange dude in Washington Square Park had no idea what a good subject he'd picked for his casual prophecy.

She wiped her face on a towel. Here she was, stuck in camp with eight plus weeks to go. She vowed to herself to try to make the most of it.

5

Reena

Great, Reena thought. *I've just been stranded in the woods*. Following Nathan's example, she tried to hold it together.

Lila led her down a wide dirt path that ran through the center of the camp, the dining hall and lake on one side, and two circles of brown wooden cabins, one for boys and one for girls, on the other. Lila gave hugs and cheek kisses to boys and girls along the dirt path, sometimes shouting with glee at the sight of a particular friend. At first she introduced Reena like this: "This is my cousin Reena," after which Reena did her best to make eye contact and smile, the two rules of successful communication according to her dad. She felt like a toad.

After the third introduction Lila seemed to tire of the routine and then Reena just stared off in the distance while Lila did her hugging and kissing. She saw a dusty baseball diamond, basketball and tennis courts, dozens of wooden cabins with green roofs and windows covered with stapled screens. She saw children in shorts and t-shirts, walking purposefully from here to there, clearly knowing what was here and what was there. Lila kept talking and talking and Reena stood there waving her hand back and forth in front of her face to keep the gnats away from her eyes. And then without warning Lila would move on and Reena would grab her bags and follow her along the dirt path.

The cabin itself was dark and smelled of old wood and Lysol. Beside one of a half dozen bunk beds Reena found her army duffle, which had been magically delivered from her apartment. Exhausted from the trip and the heat, she flopped down onto the bottom bunk's plastic-covered mattress, making the metal springs creak. The bottom bunk felt like a hiding place, which she liked. She lay down and took out her cell phone, to see if maybe her father had texted her.

"Aha. The mystery bunkmate arrives." The bed quivered as the source of the voice jumped to the floor. Reena dropped the phone as a girl thrust a hand in her face. "Hi. Sharon Jacobi-Baum. Consider yourself warned. Neatness is not my forte." Reena shook her hand and sat up.

"You must be Reena," she added.

Sharon looked Reena up and down, so Reena did the same to her. She was a short stocky girl with straight dirty-blond hair parted in the middle. Reena ran her fingers through her wild curls, trying in vain to tame them.

"I'm Lila's cousin," she said, in explanation.

"So I've heard," Sharon said. "Interesting."

"What? Why is that interesting?"

"Never mind," Sharon said. "I took the top cubbies. You can have those four there. Oh, and make sure you hide your cell phone pronto or the counselors will confiscate it. It won't do you any good here, anyway. There's no service for miles in any direction."

Reena felt her spirits alternately rise and fall. She liked Sharon's spunkiness and friendliness. But no cell phones! She felt more isolated than ever.

More girls came inside to unpack. Reena recognized some of the faces from the photo in Lila's room, including a girl with a dark, pin-straight ponytail and closely set eyes. That girl and some of the others rushed outside when a few boys showed up on the porch. Reena saw Lila through the screen window, blowing a giant bubble in the face of a boy with a mop of brown hair covering his eyes. He pushed Lila, and she pretended to fall down, giggling all the while. But then a tall blonde boy walked up the steps, and Lila turned her attention to him. The blonde kid whispered in the ear of the straight-pony girl, and Lila leaned in, trying to be part of it. All the kids were crowding around those two. All except the mop-headed boy, who retreated to the back of the group as if he had other things on his mind. Reena wondered who he was.

"My best friend, Sarah, didn't come back this summer," Sharon said.

"How come?" Reena asked, putting a stack of her t-shirts onto a shelf.

"Her family moved to California." Sharon was unpacking a bag full of books. "It really sucks. She was supposed to be my bunkmate."

"I'm sorry." Reena realized Sharon thought she had to explain why she wasn't bunking with a friend. She thought it might make her feel better to know that things hadn't exactly gone her way either.

"My dad went to Japan without me," she said. "He's on tour with his band."

"Like a rock band?"

"No, jazz."

"Oh, I like jazz. My dad has lots of Miles Davis records."

"Mine, too."

"So did your mom go with him?"

"No, I don't have a mom." She could see the questions in Sharon's face. She'd found it was easier to get it out at the beginning. "She died when I was a baby."

"How did she die?"

Reena was surprised. Most people were afraid to ask.

"She had an aneurysm. It's when a blood vessel in your brain explodes."

Sharon was quiet for a minute, thinking. "Life is unfair," she said finally.

"It's okay."

"No, it's not. Sometimes I hate my mother, but still I'm glad I have one."

Reena took her toiletries out of her duffle bag, and said, "Sometimes I hate mine too."

—

Their counselor, Susie, woke everyone up by walking around the room and tapping their feet. "Wakey wakey," she said over and over in a scratchy, tired voice.

Reena had been in camp for seven days, but it felt like seven months. "That's camp time for you," Sharon had told her—"super-slow and then over before you know it." Sharon had turned out to be the perfect guide—her mother was the camp's assistant director, which made her a "staff brat." She'd been raised at camp.

Sharon swung her legs down from the top bunk just as Reena was starting to get out of bed. She felt Sharon's feet touch her head, so she sat back down. Sharon jumped to the ground and fell on her bed next to her, and they started laughing. Sharon had a way of making her laugh. She could just raise an eyebrow and Reena would get hysterical. The day before, they were at arts and crafts making collages out of old magazines, and Sharon had made these hilarious creatures with human heads and duck bodies. She'd made speech bubbles for them, too: "Quack off!" and "You like my eggs?" They were laughing so hard that tears dripped onto their collages.

"Come on, girls, no more goofing around," Susie said. "Get dressed! *T'filot* in fifteen minutes!"

Reena stood up and pulled on a blue bathing suit and then shorts, t-shirt, and a mint-green hooded sweatshirt. In the first few days of camp, she felt like she was doing everything wrong—she wore jeans one morning, and had to go back to the cabin to change an hour later because she was so sweaty. But Sharon had set her straight. "Always dress for 100 degree weather," she'd said, "and wear layers in the morning if it's cold." She also told Reena that arts and crafts was the best elective, and to avoid radio and nature. She showed her shortcuts around camp, and told her stories about things that had happened in previous summers—like once a counselor was fired for smoking behind the cabin.

"Smoking what?" Reena asked.

That made Sharon laugh. "Cigarettes, you goof."

They set off together for the first activity of the day. The routine was already as familiar to Reena as a catchy jingle: a rotating schedule of sports, art, singing, eating, swimming and praying. Yes, praying. Every morning before breakfast, and every evening before returning to our cabins, they had *t'filot*. Strangely enough, she was already beginning to get used to it.

They arrived at the multi-purpose space called the *Beitan*. The room, if you could call it that, had no walls —just a rectangular poured-concrete floor and a high slanted roof propped on metal beams. The campers from the three girls' cabins and three boys' cabins in their division shuffled in and sank sleepily onto rows of backless benches arranged in a semi-circle. One of the boys' counselors stood with a serious boy named Matt beside a podium in the center. "Page 8," the counselor announced, and seventy campers opened their worn red *siddurs*, while Matt led everyone in the opening prayer, "*Ma Tovu.*"

Sharon sang; Reena hummed. If you didn't know better, you might think that *t'filot* was a sing-along. Every prayer had a tune, and the tunes were the kind that got stuck in your head, so even if you couldn't read Hebrew, and had never said a prayer in your life, you found yourself humming along, singing without meaning to.

Reena had never seen anything like this before she came to camp—kids her own age holding Hebrew prayer books, swaying and singing, standing and sitting. Her father avoided synagogue at all costs, so she'd only been on the high holidays with Grandma and Zeyde. And when she thought about those visits, all she could remember were adults listening intently to an elderly rabbi with a deep voice. She couldn't remember any young people at all—except running around in the hallways outside the sanctuary.

Of course, she and her father had attended synagogue for Lila's bat mitzvah. How uncomfortable her dad had looked during the endless praying, with Lila's pink leather bat-mitzvah yarmulke falling off his head! Lila, wearing a couture dress and heels, read from the Torah, and gave a speech about her tzedakah project: collecting used suits and dresses so the needy could look stylish at job interviews.

Reena knew that Grandma had been disappointed that she didn't have a bat mitzvah. Grandma even offered to orchestrate one for her at her synagogue. But Reena had felt the way she assumed her father did: that it wasn't for her. Praying was something she did when she felt anxious or worried, like when she was swimming in the ocean and got slammed under by a forceful wave. But it was silent and personal, almost like dreaming. It was nothing like saying actual prayers.

Here at camp most kids really knew the prayers; but that didn't mean they always said them. Lots of kids just stood there holding their *siddurs* open to their chests and daydreamed. Others chatted under their breath to their neighbors until, every now and then, a counselor would turn around and shush them. Reena probably would have been one of the chatters, too, if it hadn't been for Sharon. She was the only one that she felt like talking to, but she didn't talk during prayers; she actually said them.

Sharon wore a *tallis* and *tefillin* like the boys. Except the boys had no choice: they had to wear them, but for girls it was optional. Sharon was one of only a handful of girls in their division that chose to wear them.

When it came time for the *Amidah*, the silent prayer, everyone stood. Reena watched as Sharon swayed in her purple-striped *tallis*, the little black boxes of her *tefillin* tied to her arm and head with black leather straps. Her lips moved as she read the Hebrew words to herself. Reena assumed the other kids must think she was weird—who did she think she was—a rabbi? But Sharon wasn't stuck-up. Her mom sometimes came to their services, and she also wore *tallis* and *tefillin*. *If my mom were around*, Reena thought, *I'd probably do whatever she did, too*. To her credit, Sharon didn't seem bothered about what other people thought, one way or the other. She just did what she wanted to, and in that way she was a bit of a punk. It made Reena like her more.

Shifting her weight from foot to foot, Reena flipped through the pages in the prayer book without looking at them. She stared into the woods behind the Beitan as her mind wandered.

She thought about her father. She imagined him living it up in Japan, playing music till dawn and being served tea by geishas.

She thought about her mother. She wondered if she had stood in this same space when she was in camp. She thought about the photos of her at camp, and of the strange man with the beard. She didn't want to believe what Lila had told her, that her mother had been a big flirt, had maybe even been in love with someone else. But in truth she knew almost nothing about her parents' lives before they had her.

She thought about Lila. Her cousin had barely spoken to her since they'd stepped out of Aunt Mara's car; not that Reena was surprised about that. She saw Lila whispering with her friends in the back row of benches. Lila looked up and saw Reena watching her; then she laughed and looked down at her *siddur*. Reena turned away and fanned herself with her hand, feeling overheated. Were they talking about her?

She looked at her watch and sighed: still twenty minutes until breakfast. Needing a break, she put her *siddur* down on the bench and made a quick exit. She headed in the direction of the girls' cabins so the counselors, if they noticed, would think she was just going to the bathroom.

She needed to breathe, and some space to herself. She remembered seeing the start of a path into the woods behind G-5. She decided it would be okay to have a quick look—she'd be right back, and no one would miss her. With all the campers in services, and no shrieking or music coming from the cabins, she could hear her feet crunching on twigs and leaves as she walked along the trail.

—

Reena ran down the path, wanting to see where it was headed, feeling like an explorer. As the bushes on either side of the path grew thicker, she moved the brush out of her way and stepped over thick roots and rocks. She wondered what poison ivy looked like. The path turned and went uphill, and she realized that this must be the hill that you could see in the distance from the sports fields. It was still early, and she could tell that it would be a hot day; the sun shone fiercely through the trees.

After a few minutes the path leveled out and she found herself in a sunny clearing. She sat down on a tree that must have fallen down in a storm, and looked up at the sky. The canopy of treetops made an intricate design backlit by the sun, like the doilies her grandmother wore in her hair to synagogue.

There was something about this place that felt sacred. It made her think of the tiny Hindu chapel she and her dad had visited when they'd gone to see his friend on an ashram in Colorado. There were flowers, incense, and a wall of glimmering statues of gods and goddesses on pedestals. Though she found it hard to believe that her dad's friend actually prayed to the statues, she couldn't deny the feeling of calm and warmth that she'd felt there. It was the same, here.

She heard the crackling sound of footsteps and felt the urge to hide. So much for solitude. But the clearing was surrounded on all sides by tightly-packed brush and trees with gnarled roots; there was no place to go.

A man appeared. He didn't walk—he skipped, or danced, as if his movements were timed to music. A blond beard hung down several inches from the tip of his chin. A tweed cap covered his straggly hair, and his blue eyes sparkled in the sun. He wore crumpled black trousers, a white shirt, and a raggedy striped vest several sizes too big for his skinny frame. His feet were bare.

What a strange-looking counselor, she thought. She didn't know what he wanted, and her heart thumped.

"Welcome," he said, his eyes wide and unblinking.

She looked in all directions to see if he might be speaking to someone else, though she knew there was no one else around.

"Thanks," she said, wondering, to where?"

"To this place, at this time," he said. "Remember: 'to lose one's way is to find another.'"

Oh my god, she thought, *do they have crazy homeless guys in the country too?* And then she remembered all the talk in the cabin at night about Hudson Valley State Institution, on the other side of the lake. Every ghost story told in camp involved the place and its patients—or inmates.

Fear creeping up her neck, she remembered her street smarts. She was fourteen, and a city kid born and bred. She knew how to deal with crazies. Keep your distance. Avoid confrontation. Get away.

But she was cornered, as he was standing at the entrance to the path. She couldn't get away without first getting closer to him. And then he did something that stopped her frozen.

He started singing. There were no words, just a circular melody sung in a repetitive, rhythmic lilt. There was something about his tune that was entrancing. He didn't sing like a crazy person. He sang with feeling, like a musician. Also, his song was somehow familiar. Had she heard this song before? Perhaps so long ago that she couldn't fully remember?

He danced closer and closer to where she sat. *Beware*, she thought: *I'm being seduced.* Her dad always said: 'Don't trust men, especially sweet-talkers.' What about sweet-singers?

Then he leaned on the log beside her and opened the burlap sack that he carried over his shoulder. Removing a triangular chunk of dark brown bread from his bag, he held it out to her in his weather-worn palm.

Though it looked delicious, wholesome and real, unlike the camp cafeteria food she'd been eating, and though she was hungry, having yet to eat breakfast, she shook her head.

"No, thank you," she said. Of course she couldn't take his food. How did she know he wasn't trying to poison her? If he wasn't an evil escapee, he certainly looked poor. What if that bread was all he had to eat for a week?

He bowed his head, and then held the bread up to the sky and intoned, "*Baruch atah adonai eloheinu melech ha'olam hamotzi lechem min ha'aretz.*"

Reena had been hearing this blessing three times a day for the week she'd already been at camp, so she knew by then what it was for—it was the blessing over bread, said before every meal. But she'd never heard it sung before, not like that. His voice had the clear, warm sound of the jazz singers on her father's old records. It was the sound of an original.

Just as he finished the blessing, there was a clap of thunder in the distance. The sky went dark.

"I need to go," she said.

"Go in peace," he replied.

She started jogging down the path, but she could hear him humming, the sound as loud in her ears as it had been when she was standing right next to him. She turned around. She didn't worry that he would follow and attack her like in the horror stories the girls told at night to scare each other. She wondered who he was, and where he had come from. And even though it felt wrong to think it, she couldn't help hoping she'd see him again.

6

Naomi

"One, two, three, lift!" Jay, the head lifeguard, instructed.

Naomi, Jay, Jennifer, and Greg lifted a five-by-eight-foot metal raft from the pile beside the lake where they were kept through the off-season.

"Don't drop it on my toes!" Jennifer pleaded.

"Doing my best!" Naomi replied. She inched backwards towards the water's edge in baby steps. The raft was heavy and awkward; she struggled to keep a grip on it. A few more feet and they could slip it in the water.

"Come on, ladies, this doesn't need to take all day!" said Greg, who had the advantage of moving forwards.

"You being a pain in the neck won't make us go any faster," said Jennifer.

At last Naomi felt her heels touch the cool water. She and Jennifer continued to back up, lowering their end onto the surface of the lake and moving out of the way as Greg and Jay gave their end a push. Raft number one was in the water. The day was just getting started.

Many counselors considered Staff Week the best part of the summer—with no campers and the responsibilities that came with them, camp was their playground. But as far as Naomi was concerned, it was a week of backbreaking labor.

Once they got the other rafts in, they would have to tow them out to their assigned spots to form the swimming area, and anchor them with cinderblocks and rope. There were also sailboats and rowboats to set up, life jackets to clean and organize, first aid equipment to collect and arrange, and emergency drills that terrified Naomi to the core.

Earlier that morning there'd been a search-and-rescue drill. Four lifeguards lined up in the deep water and dove repeatedly to the bottom, ten feet down, as Jay barked at them. When Naomi finally spotted the submerged "victim" in the form of an orange traffic cone, it took her three dives to pull it off the muddy lake bottom. She came up with the slippery, awkward thing and pulled it to shore, where Jay was lying, now the victim. She did her best to remember the emergency procedure. "Call an ambulance!" she yelled, and rolled Jay over to pretend to clear his lungs.

Half-way through this enactment, Jay sat up and said, not just to her but to the whole waterfront staff who were standing around watching, "I just want you to know that if I weren't dead already from being at the bottom of the lake for ten minutes, Naomi just killed me."

Naomi swallowed hard as she listened to Jay's criticism. She could take it, rotten as it was.

Now, lugging rafts, she had to remind herself why she had decided to take this job in the first place—because the lake was her favorite place in camp; because every camper's favorite person is their swimming teacher; because she and Jennifer had decided to take the lifeguarding course together, so that they could work together.

Once the other rafts were in the water, Naomi and Jennifer used a rowboat to deliver the cinderblock anchors, one for each corner. "Here," Jennifer said, lifting a cinderblock out of the rowboat.

Naomi kneeled at the edge of the raft and took it from her, wincing in her effort to keep hold of it. "Got it."

"I need a bathroom break. I'll be back in a few, and I'll bring the rest of the blocks."

"Okay, I'll be here."

Naomi watched Jennifer row towards shore, and then leaned back on the raft. She was glad to have the next ten minutes to rest in the sun. When Jennifer came back they would tie long ropes to the cinderblocks and to the edge of the raft before dropping the anchors into the deep water; their fingers would soon be raw from lifting and tying.

The sun felt glorious on her wet skin. She kept perfectly still, feeling the breeze whip over her and listening to the sound of the water lapping against the raft. She hoped it wasn't drifting too far—otherwise she'd have to get in the water and swim it back.

She thought about the many summers she'd spent at camp. As a young girl she'd been very shy, and hardly said a word at school, but she'd felt like a different person at camp. There, she had close friendships forged over eight weeks of sleeping, eating, and playing together in close quarters. She had friends that she only saw during the summer, and yet each summer they picked up like no time had gone by. She smiled thinking about those early years —the little dramas that filled their days when they were nine, ten, eleven. She remembered the thrill of Color War, and the excitement of camping night, when they ate potatoes roasted in the fire and slept in sleeping bags under the stars. Camp was where Naomi had learned to French-braid hair, and make lanyard bracelets, and dance in circles like an Israeli.

She took a deep breath and let the air seep through her teeth. She couldn't help thinking that she was missing out on something this summer, like she did as a child when she was sent to bed early while her parents entertained downstairs. She had met people in the city who were artists, activists, and thinkers. They were doing things right now—they were gathering and organizing, creating and learning; forging a world that they wanted to live in. And what was she doing? Spending her summer secluded in the woods with several hundred children.

Hearing a whistle coming from the beach, Naomi stirred from her thoughts. It blew again. On the third blow she sat up, squinting, and looked towards the sound. Realizing that her rest time was over, she stood up. She didn't see Jennifer, who still hadn't returned with the cinderblocks. Jay was waving both hands over his head. He pointed at a tall man standing beside him and then gestured at Naomi. He must want her to give this guy a swim test. She gave the thumbs up.

The guy walked out onto the dock that led away from the beach, and she beckoned, motioning for him to swim out to her. Everyone, even the counselors and staff, had to pass a test in order to gain permission to swim in the deep area. It was a formality, really, but Jay was the type who upheld the law.

As she watched the man approach, Naomi found she didn't recognize him. Kitchen staff, she wondered? The people on kitchen staff were usually townies looking for seasonal work. They didn't socialize with the rest of the camp staff, and never once had she seen them swim in this part of the lake. He had shoulder-length straight hair, broad shoulders, and long pale legs emerging from red swim shorts. She could see the outline of his muscles the way you can with thin men, but she could tell he wasn't an athlete. It looked like it might be his first day outside all summer, from the sheen of his pallid skin.

He seemed to hesitate for a few seconds, but then dove in and swam a confident crawl stroke directly out to the raft.

"Hi. I'm Jim," he said, panting slightly as he treaded water. "What do you want me to do?"

Standing above him, Naomi felt exposed. He was looking up at her, had a full view of her stubbly thighs, her breasts taut in last summer's faded swimsuit, but all she could see was the top of his head.

"Come on up," she said, glancing towards the beach to see if Jay was watching. He wasn't.

There was no ladder, so Jim kicked and pushed up with his arms, which Naomi now saw were stronger than the rest of him, and flipped his body around quickly so that he was sitting on the edge of the raft. *Almost graceful*, Naomi thought, impressed, having seen countless kids flail themselves over the sides of rafts like beached seals.

"You want to take the swim test, I presume?" she said.

"Well, I'm told that's what's required if I want to swim in this here lake. And seeing as I do, yes."

"Great. You passed."

"Really?" he said. "Well that's a relief."

She looked at him, trying to see if he was mocking her. His eyes were deep green, like the surface of the lake.

"Yes, really. Although I will have to watch you swim two laps to that buoy over there, just because that's Jay's rule." She pointed across the swim area.

"Now?"

"If you like," she answered. She wished he would stay awhile, though she had no real reason to keep him out there on the raft with her. She looked carefully but casually at his long torso and neck. How nice for her that Jennifer had left.

"What were you doing out here before I arrived?" he asked.

She thought about saying, "waiting for you," and blushed. What was coming over her? "Just thinking," she said.

He looked at her and smiled, and seemed to be chuckling silently. Naomi noticed his bottom teeth were crooked and found the look endearing.

"What's funny?" she said.

"It's just that, it seems like you lifeguards get to loll around in the sun all day, and I'm thinking maybe I've got the wrong job here."

"What are you doing at camp?" she asked, hoping she didn't sound rude. She was very curious about him.

"I'm on the music staff. Helping with the song festival, organizing the staff and camper bands, music for plays, all that stuff."

"I didn't even know we had a music staff."

"Well, I'm it, actually. Along with Rivka, who will be teaching Israeli songs. I don't actually know any Hebrew."

She couldn't fathom why someone who had never been a camper there would choose to come, but she decided to stop asking questions. She'd been told that she asked too many. Seeing Jay looking at them, Naomi stood up.

"Whenever you're ready," she said, holding her hand out over the water.

"Whenever you say," he answered, standing up and looking in her eyes.

She looked away, aware of the closeness of their barely-clad bodies. Then she nodded, meaning, now is fine.

Jim slid into the water and turned around to face her. "You didn't tell me your name."

"Naomi," she said. "Good luck."

He shot off, his arms flying out of the black water by his side and back into it above his head.

"Nice job," she said, when he returned to the raft after the second lap. "You can swim in now—I'll let Jay know that you passed."

"Thanks. See you around?"

She smiled and watched him swim back.

The rest of the day, while tying knots and lugging boats, Naomi couldn't stop thinking about Jim. He reminded her of some of the guys she'd met at school —the ones who smoked in cafes and wrote poetry. These were the men she increasingly found herself drawn to. She hated her tendency to fall for men so quickly. She made rash judgments, knowing within minutes of meeting someone if she was interested in finding out what their lips tasted like. She knew it wasn't a good way to be; there were probably many good guys she didn't give a chance to because of her quick assessments. And besides, she reminded herself, she wasn't looking for a man. But she couldn't help it—nothing beat the electric connection. And after their short, wet meeting, she knew that she wanted to taste Jim.

At the end of the day, Naomi and Jennifer organized band-aids in the small lakeside first-aid hut known affectionately as "The Shack." Sand and dirt pricked the skin on the backs of Naomi's damp legs as she sat on the floor in her bathing suit.

"What are you smiling about?" Jennifer asked.

"Nothing," Naomi said. She hadn't realized she'd been smiling, but now she had to suppress the urge to jump up and shout. She wasn't thinking only of Jim; she was also remembering the guy in the park, the one who told her to follow her heart. Maybe there was nothing she could do about it; maybe love was in her cards.

7

Reena

Reena's division had instructional swimming right after breakfast. The morning chill was still in the air as they shuffled in their flip-flops down the steep stone steps to the lakefront.

As she walked, dragging her towel, Reena couldn't stop thinking about what had happened that morning in the woods. She had been taking a walk, finding a moment of solitude, when the strangest guy had appeared, with his beard and blue eyes, odd clothes, and voice like a clear bell. And the bizarre things he said: "To lose one's way is to find another." It sounded like one of Aesop's fables. He was from a different world. It didn't make any sense. Her father, feeling obliged to give her a drug talk, had once told her about a friend of his who had had a bad acid trip, and slept in the bathtub murmuring strange things for a week. She considered if something in her environment could have triggered a hallucination. But she hadn't eaten anything strange, nor, like that ex-counselor she'd heard about, had she smoked anything.

She decided not to tell anyone about the man in the woods. Not even Sharon, although she felt sure she could trust her. Sharon knew everything about camp, and part of her worried that Sharon have some sensible explanation for what she'd seen. Something like, "Oh, that guy? He's a charity case who's been working maintenance here for like twenty years. He says the strangest things, doesn't he?" But the rest of her worried Sharon would simply think she was crazy, so she thought it best to keep it to herself.

The kids in her division sat huddled in their towels on the sand beach, grouped into swim classes. Reena was in the advanced swim class, thanks to years of Sunday mornings swimming at the Y with her dad. It was the only exercise he could tolerate, because of a bad knee. So he'd put her in lessons and swam laps on the other side of the pool, until she could swim well enough to do the laps with him. In the summers, they sometimes visited friends on Fire Island, and they'd swim laps in the bay. Swimming was the only thing in camp for which she actually felt prepared.

Reena sat next to the girl named Michael, who was on a swim team on Long Island. Also in the group was Gail, who was perpetually complaining about the creatures living in the lake. Then there were two boys named Sam and Jeff who were always talking about baseball and spent most of their free time sailing. And lastly, sitting directly behind her, was Ethan, the mop-headed boy whom she'd noticed that first day by the porch. Reena stopped herself from turning around to look at him.

She'd heard that Ethan and Lila had hooked up last summer, but she didn't know if she believed it. Lila seemed more interested in Dan, the tall blond boy who was Mr. Popular.

"Good morning!" said Ellen, their perky instructor. "Time to warm up. We're heading out to the deep raft for laps to the outer buoy. Everyone up!"

Ellen led them in stretches and jumping jacks, and then they followed her on to the H-shaped metal dock that led out from the beach. As they passed the classes that had their instruction in shallower water, Reena saw Lila sitting on the edge of the dock, her knees tucked under her arms. She saw Sharon, too, wincing as she stuck a toe in the water. Sharon smiled, and Reena waved. Shivering in the breeze, she wrapped her arms around her chest. She felt exposed standing in her suit without any way to cover up.

"Two at a time, swim straight out," Ellen instructed. The rafts in the deep swimming area were arranged in a semi-circle. Ellen pointed to the wooden deep raft, the furthest one, situated at twelve o'clock.

"It's not healthy to swim in water this cold, you know!" said Michael, to no one in particular. "This camp needs a frickin' pool." She grabbed Gail's hand and they moved to the back of the line.

Ellen tapped Ethan and Reena and they dove into the black water without acknowledging each other. The cold was a shock, and there was only one way to warm up: swim. Reena swam hard and fast, carefully lifting each arm out of the water and kicking smoothly, breathing only every two strokes. She could feel her body moving through warm and cool pockets of water. She arrived quicker than she expected to, and at the same moment as Ethan. She had forgotten he was beside her.

"You're in a hurry today," he said.

"It's just because it's cold."

"Nah, it's because you're on fire." He smiled at her.

He climbed up the ladder and sat on the raft, and she followed. She didn't know what to say to him.

"Wow, now that's cold," he said, wrapping his arms around his chest.

She knew what he meant. Even though it was sunny and the sky was blue, the wind gusting over the lake and onto her wet body made her wish she had a towel. It felt warmer in the water.

Ethan started hopping up and down on the raft, yelling, "Come on, you slow pokes, get out here, we're freezing!" His wet hair was slicked back so she could finally see his smooth skin and round, brown eyes. Water dripped down his goose-bumped back and onto his green-and-blue-striped swim shorts.

Reena realized she was staring, and made herself look away towards the others approaching in the water. Once everyone had arrived, they jumped back in. The task was to swim laps to the red and white buoy floating in the choppy water, about fifty yards away from the back of the raft. They had done this before, and there were some groans of complaint, but not from Reena. She loved swimming out in the open lake because from there you couldn't see any part of camp at all. All you could see were the water, and the clouds, and the tree-covered hills that met the lake on the opposite shore. It was much nicer than swimming in a crowded city pool, where you had to share your lane with lots of people, and wear goggles to keep the chemicals out of your eyes. Out in the lake, she didn't even notice the other kids swimming beside her. She got into a rhythm and all she could hear was the splashing of water.

They did laps of crawl, backstroke, breaststroke, and sidestroke. On the return laps, she could hear Ellen say, "Elbows higher!" or "Kick from the hip!" At the end of class, they raced in pairs back to the shallow area. She was with Ethan again, the other four in the class being perpetually paired off. They dove off the raft at the same time. By this time she was good and warm, and felt energized rather than tired. She swam as cleanly and as efficiently as she could, looking up now and then to make sure she was taking a straight line to the dock. As she touched it and came up for air, she felt something warm on her shoulder. It sent shivers through her. She turned around and saw that it was Ethan.

"Seriously, it's like you've got jets today," he said. And then he let go, and lifted himself onto the dock with his arms in one fast motion. She swam around the side and waited until he turned around and headed towards the beach before she climbed up the slimy ladder. As she walked, dripping, back to her towel, she could still feel the place where his hand had touched her shoulder. Had he meant to do that? Or had it been a mistake, a blind reaching-out for the dock but he caught her instead?

After swimming, Sharon and Reena trudged

slowly up the waterfront steps. They had their towels around their bodies and their bunched-up clothes in their hands. A group of boys rushed past them, bounding up the steps two at a time. One of them nearly knocked Sharon over.

"Hey, watch out," she said.

"Sorry, Missus Baum," said Jonny, a chubby kid who Reena's dad would have called a smart aleck. "Please don't tell your mom on us!"

Hisses came from his friends. Reena noticed Ethan wasn't laughing. Sharon grabbed her arm and began to pull her away.

Then Dan pushed through the group of boys. "Come on, you jerks," he said. "Can you be gentlemen?" And then to Sharon: "Sorry for their stupid-ass behavior."

Jonny gave him the finger. But Dan just shrugged and smiled. *It must be nice to be that confident*, Reena thought.

At the top of the steps, Ethan caught up with Reena and Sharon. He walked beside them, like he had something to say, but didn't say anything. As he turned to go to the boys' circle, he said, "See you 'round, Reena, and um, Sharon."

On their walk back to the cabin, Sharon said, "What's with Ethan Marcus?"

"What do you mean?"

"I saw you two talking on the deep raft. I think he likes you."

"Oh, come on. He does not."

"Maybe it's a 'cousins' thing." Sharon chuckled and kicked a rock at their cabin's stoop. *Just what I need, something to make Lila hate me even more,* Reena thought as she pulled open the creaky door. She doubted Ethan Marcus liked her, anyway. Although she wondered if Sharon could be right; she seemed to be right about so many other things.

—

They changed out of their suits in the modest camp method that Reena had just recently mastered. It was nothing like the Y locker room, where ladies of every body type—skinny, fat, hard and sagging—walked around from shower to hair dryer to dressing on wooden benches, in the stark nude. The camp method went like this. Pull straps down from shoulders. With towel wrapped around body under armpits, shimmy top of suit down to belly-button. Pull on t-shirt over towel. Keeping towel around waist, tug and/or kick suit off from bottom. Pull underpants on. Drop towel and pull on shorts. All this was done as quickly as possible, over sticky, still-damp skin.

Though Reena found the whole routine a bit of a pain and missed the privacy of her own room, of course she did the bathing-suit shimmy. Everyone did. Everyone, that is, except Margaret. Margaret just pulled the whole suit off, exposing her pointy round breasts, Jell-o tummy, and triangle of gnarled pubic hair to the rest of the cabin. Margaret's bed was right next to hers, so Reena had to turn around every time Margaret was changing to give her some semblance of privacy. Truly, Reena didn't want to see. But also, she didn't want Margaret or anyone else to think she was watching. The problem was Margaret was awfully slow about the whole process.

"Geez, Mags, would you put those pubes away?" came a voice from across the cabin. The voice belonged to Allie, whose straight locks were, as always, pulled back in the slickest of ponytails. Reena remembered what Sharon had said about her: "Queen bee with a nasty sting. Stay away."

The bunk beds in the corner erupted in chuckles, and Reena recognized Lila's distinctive gravelly laugh. She couldn't understand why Lila chose to hang out with Allie.

Margaret didn't acknowledge the comment. Instead, she started humming to herself as she pulled on her flower-print underwear. Reena was blown away by how little she seemed to care what the other girls thought of her.

"Seriously, your tits are in my face," said Allie, who was always trying to get a rise out of people.

Margaret just turned around, and started sorting out her clothes on her bed.

But Allie wasn't done. She sashayed across the bunk in her towel, her perfect pony swinging from side to side, and pinched Margaret's flowered bottom.

Margaret whipped around and screamed, "You bitch! Get the hell off me!"

Allie ran back to the safety of her crew, who all fell on their beds laughing.

"Would you leave her alone?" said Sharon, coming around from the other side of their bunk bed into the middle of the floor. Though her cheeks matched her red t-shirt, her words came out steady. She stood there with her hands on her hips, daring Allie to mess with her.

"What's it to you, Sharon?" said Lila. Now Reena's cheeks went red. She didn't want Lila to be one of them.

Allie returned to the middle of the wood floor. She reveled in being the center of attention. "You and Mags want to get naked together, be our guest. But no need for a frickin' show. 'Kay?" Sharon stood her ground.

"You have no right to touch Margaret and you know it. Keep your hands to yourself, you animal."

"Whatever you say, your highness," someone said, chuckling, but Sharon didn't seem to hear it. She had already left the cabin, allowing the door to whack shut behind her.

Reena followed her. Sharon was walking fast, and it took her a minute to come up beside her, matching her strides.

"I could seriously kill Allie Berger."

"Well, no, actually, you can't," Reena said. "But she deserves it." She was trying to be supportive, although she felt small, having done nothing but watch the whole thing unravel.

They sat down in a white gazebo on the far side of the circle of girls' cabins. It was close to mid-day and the heat felt harsh. They waved gnats away from their faces.

"She used to pull that kind of shit on me when we were younger and now I can't stand it for a second."

"You're brave, you know."

"Brave? Really? Do you think it's brave to stand up to Allie Berger? Because I think it's pathetic to let her and her. . . her. . . minions do and say whatever they want. No offense to your cousin, but those girls seem to be missing brain cells."

"No, no, you're right," Reena said. And she was; Lila was pathetic. And Sharon was amazing. She reminded her of her dad, daring and willing to not care what other people thought. But still, she felt worried. Now that Sharon had so clearly called Allie out, what would happen next? Did Sharon really want to be Allie's new target? And what would happen to Reena?

8

Naomi

Naomi plugged in her curling iron to tame her lake-induced frizz. It was the final night of Staff Week; the campers would arrive the next day. She hadn't managed to spend much time with Jim since their meeting two days earlier, but she was determined to change that tonight.

She heard a knock on the door and recognized Mara's voice saying, "Naomi?"

"In here!" Naomi called, still in the bathroom.

She heard footsteps tapping on the cabin's wood floor, then the squeaking and slamming of the door to the bathroom.

"Look at you!" Mara exclaimed. "I thought you couldn't care less about the staff week dance."

Mara stood beside her and peered into the mirror. Their reflections were similar, except that Naomi was much darker. Mara's curls were tied back with a yellow ribbon, to match her yellow t-shirt. On the bottom she wore a khaki skirt. She looked like she was going to a job interview.

"I'm surprised they let you come to this," Naomi said. "No meetings for the division heads tonight?"

"Give it a rest, Naomi. I just came to see how you're doing. I know you weren't so eager to come to camp. Is it going okay?"

Naomi worked a twist of hair into the hot iron. She remembered how her mother had enlisted Mara as her spy, and she couldn't decide if Mara's checking up on her was sweet or annoying.

"I just want you to know that I'm here for you," Mara continued. "I'd do anything for you. Remember that."

"Everything's fine, Mara."

Everything was more than fine, really. The summer was getting off to a more interesting start than she had thought it could. But she wasn't about to tell Mara about Jim. She imagined with a feeling of mild nausea Mara telling their mother about him. She probably wouldn't like him. She wouldn't know his *mishpacha* and he wasn't going into medicine or law.

"There are some new cute guys on staff this summer, have you noticed?" Mara leaned an arm on the painted wooden panel between the toilet stalls.

"Who do you mean?" Naomi said.

"Look around tonight. You'll see. I already have my eye on someone."

Through the mirror Naomi saw her sister grinning and blushing. She wondered if that was why Mara had come to see her—to gloat about some boy.

"But what about Gary from the Oranges?" she asked.

"Well, he's not here, is he?"

"You're really on the prowl," Naomi murmured.

"Naomi, what is up with you?" Mara said. "You're being so . . . hostile."

Mara put her hand on Naomi's shoulder, trying to get her to turn around and face her.

Naomi turned and made herself look Mara in the eye.

"Are you angry at me?" Mara asked.

Naomi shook her head.

"But it seems like you are," Mara continued.

Naomi felt like Mara was sucking the air out of the tiny bathroom; she couldn't breathe. "I feel like you're spying on me," she said.

"What? That's absurd!"

"I feel like you're gonna call Mom and tell her everything I'm doing and who I'm talking to and every word I say all summer."

Mara's face fell. "I'm insulted. Truly, you've insulted me."

"But isn't that why they wanted me here, at camp, with you? So you could watch me?"

"No, that's not it at all. They wanted you in camp because they were afraid that in the city you'd fall in with a bad crowd. You know, druggies and pimps."

"Ah, got it. Well, I'm safe here. No pimps as far as the eye can see."

"I don't know what to do with you. You can't even have a conversation."

"I'm sorry," Naomi said. "I think I just had a stressful day on the waterfront. Too much sun or whatever."

"Did something happen? Are you ok?"

"Yeah, I'm fine. Really. Listen, I just need to finish my hair and throw something on. I'm really sorry. See you at the dance, ok?"

"Yes, see you there," Mara said, leaning in to kiss Naomi's cheek.

9

Reena

The rain began during the night, and didn't let up all day. Usually, camp was buzzing with activity, as games of basketball and softball whirled on every court and field, and groups of campers walked or skipped or ran from place to place. But camp changed in the rain. The pace slowed, as most people tried to avoid the dirt paths that turned into chocolate rivers. It made sense to stay in on rainy days at camp. Once you got wet, there was no way to dry off, because of the humidity. A wet towel could stay damp for days.

Swimming was cancelled, and the campers were free, after breakfast, to do what they wanted. Most girls hung out in the cabin and wrote letters or chatted on their beds. But Sharon had been avoiding the cabin whenever possible, now that she was public enemy number one with Allie and her friends. It had become vicious, with cold stares, snickers, and nasty exchanges daily. Throughout it all, Sharon held her head high. But what choice did she have, really? Like Reena, she was stuck in camp.

Sharon sat down on Reena's bed and whispered in her ear. "I'm going to my parents' cabin. Wanna come?"

It was the first time Sharon had invited her. She imagined her parents' cabin as a haven—a parental paradise with a large fridge full of chocolate cake, maybe, or more simply, a tiny slice of home.

Reena agreed to come, and they threw their plastic ponchos over their shorts and headed out into the monsoon. They tried to stay to the edges of the muddy paths, trudging in their sneakers through the grass. The rain whipped at their bare legs, and they held their hoods down over their eyes.

As they passed the baseball diamond, Reena glanced up at the wooded hills in the distance, which were hard to make out for all the clouds. She wondered if the mystery man in the forest was still there. She still hadn't said anything about him to Sharon. She couldn't find the right time, or the right words, to explain it. The more days that went by, the more it seemed like a daydream, a trick of her anxious mind.

It took them longer than usual to make it across camp, but finally they reached the small brown cottage near the infirmary where Sharon's mother lived, and her father too on the weekends.

They climbed the stone steps and Sharon opened the door without knocking. As they stripped off their rain gear and sneakers, Reena started to shiver. The air was cool and dry and, with her damp hair and skin, it felt like entering a refrigerator.

"Air conditioning," Sharon said. "Nice, huh?"

The room was dark and had two old plaid Salvation-Army-looking sofas in it. Sharon plopped down on one, and Reena fell into the other. The walls were made of dark wood, and were undecorated except for some window coverings made from tie-dyed sheets. It was quiet but for the whirring sound of the window unit; you could barely even hear the rain.

"Welcome to my parents' luxurious summer house. What do you think? Almost like the Hamptons, no?" Sharon smiled, and Reena laughed.

Her thoughts flashed to a sleepover at a friend's country house in Southampton, where there were eight bedrooms and only four members of the family, and the bathrooms were stocked with thick plush white towels, and there was a separate cabana by the gleaming blue-tiled pool for changing into your swimsuit. She gathered Sharon had had a similar experience. The more they got to know each other, the more Reena realized that their urban lives were similar, though Sharon lived on the Upper West Side and went to a Jewish day school and lived with two parents. Some things, like friends with summer houses, were just part of growing up in Manhattan.

Sharon went into the little kitchen and came back with two cups of sweet tea and a stack of old magazines. They sat on the sofas and sipped and talked and laughed until they heard the front door creak. Sharon's mother Anne came in, dripping. Under her poncho she wore a blue sweatshirt with the camp logo on it, and her hair was twisted in a clip at the back of her head.

"Hello, girls," she said. "Did you blow in with the storm?"

"Hi, Eema," Sharon said. "Have you seen how bad it is out there? Rivers of mud. But it's even worse inside cabin G-8."

"Yes, I know, I know." Anne sat down on a chair across from them. "It's not gotten any better yet? So how's everything going for you this summer, Reena?"

Reena guessed she was asking if she'd also been suffering at the hands of Allie and her friends. The truth was, she wasn't. She kept expecting them to turn on her; but, so far, they hadn't. Maybe, as Lila's cousin, she was off limits?

"It's been ok," she said. "I miss my dad."

"I'm sure. It's hard to be away from your parents." She looked at Sharon. "But maybe harder to be near them."

"What's that supposed to mean, Mom?" Sharon said.

"I mean, you might find these issues with your cabin-mates a bit easier to deal with if you weren't always hiding out here."

"No, I'd just be suffering more. Do you like it when I suffer?"

"You know I don't. But I know how girls can be. I was a camper too, remember."

"Yeah, about a hundred years ago."

"Not quite, Sharon. And anyway, girls were the same then. Believe me."

"Did you know my mom?" Reena asked. "She went to camp here, too. Naomi Halpern? No—I mean, Gordon?"

"Do you know when she was here?"

"No, I'm not sure."

"Well, how old is she?"

Reena thought for a moment. "She'd be forty, I think, if she were around," she said, looking at Sharon. Had Sharon not told her mother?

Then Reena saw the flash of recognition, and pity, in Anne's eyes. "Yes, yes, of course I knew her. We were here at the same time, but I'm a couple of years older. I remember working with her sister Mara—we were division heads together." Anne turned her head to the side, thinking, the way that adults sometimes did when remembering the past.

Reena winced at the mention of Aunt Mara. Imagine if Mara knew that Lila and Reena were hardly even friends.

"Wait a second, you know Lila's mom?" Sharon said. "How is it that this has never come up before?"

"Sweetheart, I know a lot of the parents of your friends. It doesn't come up if you don't ask."

Reena thought about asking Sharon's mom if she knew her dad, too. But she was afraid to ask. Maybe she knew more about her mother's other boyfriends.

—

That night after lights out, huddled under a blanket in her narrow lower bunk, Reena reached under the bed and pulled out her stationery box—an old cigar box that her dad had given her. Inside it, she kept the purple paper and envelopes with the "R" monogram at the top that her grandmother had given her for her birthday, five twenties that her dad had given her "just in case", and the pictures that she'd swiped from Lila's house on Passover. She shined her flashlight on the photos. Now she recognized the lake backdrop in the shot of Aunt Mara and her mother—the contour of the beach and trees, and the shape of the shoreline, looked surprisingly the same, though so much time had passed. She flipped to the image of Mara and her father. It was strange to see them look so happy together. Was it possible that they had once been friends? What had happened between them? The last picture was the one of her mother, with that man standing behind her.

"Oh. My. God." Reena sat up, throwing the covers over her head. She didn't know his name, but she was pretty sure it was him. She could hear the sound of his sweet singing, engraved in her memory like his image was fixed in the photo.

Friday afternoon came and camp was a flurry of activity as everyone prepared for Shabbat. In cabin G-8 girls were running around half-dressed, trying on each other's clothes and primping in front of the mirror. There were shouts coming from the bathroom —"Holy cow! This is freezing!"—there was never any hot water on Fridays when the whole camp was trying to shower at the same time. They were all meant to be cleaning up the cabin, too. After she finished sweeping the floor—her job that day on the chore chart—Reena took a thirty-second icy shower, and put on a jean skirt and a white t-shirt with a scoop neck. There was a rule that you had to wear white for Shabbat. Since everything was upside down and hectic, and Sharon wasn't around—she'd gone to get ready in her mother's cabin—Reena decided to go for a walk.

At first, when she started up the path, all she could hear was music and shouting from the girls' circle, but soon those sounds became fainter until all she could hear was the sound of her sandals crunching on twigs. She came to the fallen tree, and sat down, crossing her ankles. He'll come, she thought, if I wait.

She'd never believed in anything she couldn't see or touch, other than the constancy of her dad. And even that was on shaky ground, with him having abandoned her for the summer. But she believed, with a strange conviction, that the singing man she'd met in the clearing would come back again.

As she sat there, Reena thought about her mother. She imagined her mom as she looked in the photos, happy and young, but serious. Purposeful. Beautiful. Of course lots of men loved her. But Reena's brain spun when she considered the story Lila had told her. Maybe the man in the photograph was one of the guys that her mother had been involved with? But where did that leave her dad? And who was the man she'd met here in the woods?

She heard rustling and sat up straight. Footsteps on the path. She didn't look; she gazed up at the trees and the sky, as if deep in contemplation.

"Hey, Reena. I see you've found my favorite place in camp."

She felt blood rush to her head when she turned around and saw that it was Ethan. He was wearing blue shorts and a Yankees t-shirt, and was carrying an acoustic guitar.

"Hi," she said. It was all she could manage.

"Do you mind if I play guitar?"

She shook her head, and he sat down on the log, a few feet away. Was it true, what Sharon had said, that he liked her? It didn't seem possible. And anyway, she wasn't sure she liked him. He was always hanging around his group of rowdy friends, like Dan the Man and Jonny Bernstein, who had nearly pushed Sharon over that morning on the waterfront steps, and who, the day before, had taunted *"renal failure!"* when Reena missed a fly ball in a softball game. Her dad said you could usually get a good idea of a person's character from their friends, so she wasn't sure what to think about Ethan.

But she hadn't known that he played guitar. He

started plucking at the strings, playing this and that until he settled into a chord progression. He wasn't bad—his fingers moved smoothly over the frets. Maybe it was the place, the sweet air of the woods, or maybe it was her memory of the man she'd met there, who had sung spontaneously in that same spot, but something made her want to sing. She looked at him, wondering what he would think if she did.

At first she hummed, and then she started singing, not words but just sounds that seemed to work. It was something she'd seen jazz singers do all her life, something she and her dad would do together while making dinner, or in the car. Ethan smiled at her, and nodded his approval. She nervously peeled bark off the log she was sitting on as she sang.

"I haven't sung like that since I've been here," she said, brushing off her hands. She looked up at the sky through the trees. She couldn't look at Ethan directly.

"You're really good," he said. "Where did you learn to do that?"

"I guess that's what happens when you're raised on Ella and Dinah. My dad and I always sing together."

"Sounds like a good way to be raised. All my parents ever listen to is talk radio."

"So how did you learn to play guitar?"

"My older brother taught me a few chords, and then I just got a book and worked on it. My mom says I spend too much time alone."

"You never seem to be alone," she said, thinking of Dan and Jonny.

"What's that supposed to mean?"

"Nothing, forget it," she said. She'd liked singing with him. She felt like she had to say the right thing, so that he'd know that. "I like to be alone, too."

"Well I won't tell anyone I saw you here."

"I won't either," she said.

"I should probably get going. One more song?"

Reena nodded. This was so unexpected, and yet felt so natural. Singing in the woods with Ethan, her swim buddy. *There really must be something in the air up here,* she thought.

"You pick one."

She started singing: "Sometimes I lay under the moon/ And I thank God I'm breathing."

"Hold on, I know this," he said. He worked out the chords and then they sang the song together. Laughing, they both did their best reggae voices. Then Ethan stood up.

"I have to go get ready or I'll be late for Shabbat. You coming?"

Remembering what she had originally come there for, Reena shook her head. "I think I'll stay for a few more minutes. Too crazy down there." She pointed towards the girls' circle. She didn't want to emerge from the woods with Ethan, anyway. Someone would see them and misunderstand.

"I don't blame you. 'Til next time on Blackberry Hill," he said, bowing in a goofy way, as he took his guitar and went down the path.

She walked in a circle around the clearing, unable to sit still. Everything that she and Ethan had just said to each other was running through her head. *What's Blackberry Hill?* she wondered. She was thinking she should probably get back to the cabin when a feeling like a cold breeze made her turn around.

"Welcome!" the bearded man said, his eyes smiling. He was wearing the same odd clothes and again no shoes, but this time his face was red, and he seemed to be out of breath. Reena felt the same. She didn't know where he'd come from. She'd watched Ethan go down the trail just minutes before. Had they seen each other?

"Do not tarry. *Shabbos* is coming!"

And with that, he danced down the path.

This time, Reena followed. She had a million questions for him. Where was he going? Where did he live? Why did she only ever see him in the woods? Why did no one else seem to know about him? And, the one that really mattered: was it possible he had known her mother? But soon she was standing at the mouth of the path between the girls' cabins; and the mystery man was nowhere in sight. Reena promised herself that the next time she saw him, she would find out who he was.

—

Coming back into the girls' circle, Reena joined the campers heading toward the basketball courts for *Kabbalat Shabbat*. The bleachers were covered in a sea of kids and counselors wearing white and smelling of shampoo. She sat with the girls from her cabin, halfway up the bleachers. Sharon had been chosen to lead the service that welcomes in the Sabbath, and was standing at half-court. When she began to sing the prayer "*L'cha Dodi*", she was joined by hundreds of voices.

Reena didn't know the words or what they meant, but still, when everyone was singing she found herself humming along. It occurred to her that an alien watching wouldn't be able to tell her apart from the other kids, even though she still felt like she hardly belonged.

But then she thought of Ethan and their jam session in the woods. She scanned the bleachers for him, wanting to see him, almost to prove that he was real. While she was looking she caught a glimpse of a figure moving in the trees at the edge of the court. Was she imagining it, or did she see the straggly blond beard and the tweed cap? The way the figure moved—he seemed to dance between the trees —made her believe it could be the man from the clearing.

She stood up. Whispering "excuse me" to the campers sitting in front of her—including Lila, who raised her eyes questioningly as she moved aside—

Reena climbed down to the ground and walked behind the bleachers. She moved quietly down the length of the court in the hidden space beneath where everyone was sitting; she could see bare calves and sandaled feet through the cracks in the benches. When she reached the edge of the court, she stared into the woods, but didn't see anyone there.

"Psst. Reena! What are you doing here?" came a voice. She turned around. Ethan, again.

"What are *you* doing here?" Reena whispered.

"I got the last shower, so just arrived," he said. "Trying to make a casual entrance." He smiled, and pushed his still-wet hair away from his eyes. "What about you?"

Reena glanced into the woods but saw nothing.

"Just stretching my legs," she said.

She could tell Ethan wasn't in a rush to join the services. She wasn't sure if she should go back to her seat. He touched the side of the dark wooden bleachers. They were covered in etchings—"R+K 4 EVA" and "Harry loves Fran" and "B-10 '83" and "Led Zep"—ancient graffiti from summers past. She had never been behind the bleachers before, and hadn't known these messages were there.

Ethan ran his fingers over the etchings as if they could tell him something about the people who left the marks. And that's when Reena noticed his fingers resting on a particular message. Without thinking, she grabbed his hand to move it, and held on to it as she read, "Jim+Naomi."

"My parents," she mumbled.

Ethan squeezed her hand. She felt dizzy, like she needed to sit. She pulled away, and retraced her steps behind the bleachers to return to her seat. She wondered if the girls all around her could hear how hard her heart was beating.

A minute later she saw Ethan come around the side of the bleachers. He slapped high fives with the boys in his cabin as he squeezed in beside them.

Services came to a close and everyone stood up and started walking across the baseball diamond and up the dusty road to the dining hall. Reena couldn't find Sharon in the crowd, so she walked to dinner with Margaret and a few of her friends.

As they neared the dining hall, Reena felt a tap on her shoulder. She turned around.

"What's up, Allie?" she said, doing her best to play it cool.

"Lila's your cousin, right?" Allie came so close to her that Reena had to be careful not to step on her perfect pink pedicure.

"Yes."

"Well, I don't know what it's like in the city, but in New Jersey we don't screw over our cousins."

"What are you talking about?" Reena said, taking several steps to the side.

Allie came closer again.

"Don't play dumb, Reena. All of camp just saw you and Ethan come out from behind the bleachers together. You really are a piece of work: not only do you steal your cousin's boyfriend, but you make sure to do it with an audience."

Reena was speechless. Was Ethan Lila's boyfriend? Had she stolen him? What was the meaning of what happened behind the bleachers?

Someone shouted Allie's name and she took off to return to her giggling friends. Reena shuffled slowly into the dining hall, hoping that Sharon had saved her a seat at her table. She needed to think. Things were starting to get complicated.

10

Naomi

Naomi stopped at Jennifer's cabin so they could walk to the dance together. It was a muggy evening; sweat collected on Naomi's forehead and under her arms. Jennifer kept her hands on her hips in an attempt to keep dry the fabric of her pink tank dress. Naomi didn't have to worry about that; she'd considered wearing a sundress but had settled instead on a black t-shirt and shorts. Better to not appear to be trying. Bonus: she could sweat, and no one would be able to tell.

They walked slowly across the softball field to the social hall, the largest building at camp other than the dining hall. The building looked from the outside like a scaled-up cabin, with the same sloping roof and simple brown wood exterior, but inside there was a basic gymnasium.

"I don't know why we go to these things," said Jennifer, as they picked up cups of red bug juice. "It'll be the same sorry excuse for music, and the same can't-dance-to-save-your-life counselors as always."

"So true," said Naomi. She struck a pose. "Yet, here we are, two hot girls on a hot summer night." Naomi walked around her friend, hands on hips. "Girl just wanna have fun, right?"

"I swear I don't recognize you right now," said Jennifer, laughing.

Naomi linked her arm in Jennifer's. "Come on."

They moved towards the stage where Mark Goldstein was setting up a drum set and Benjy Fine was tooting randomly on a clarinet. Naomi paused at the sight of Jim. He was on the stage, too, setting up a folding metal chair and sitting down with his guitar. Of course it made sense that he'd be performing, but still it hadn't occurred to her that he'd be the entertainment.

"Who's the guy with the guitar?" asked Jennifer.

"That's him, the one I told you about. From the swim test?"

"That's him, huh? Well, he's no Tom Cruise, but he's got nice arms. Too bad I missed seeing him swim!" Jennifer gently nudged Naomi on the side of her arm.

"What's that supposed to mean? You can't compare every man to Tom Cruise. There's something about him—he's got this way of making you feel like he's never met anyone so interesting as you in his life." Naomi took a sip of bug juice, and the cold liquid gave her a chill reminiscent of standing on the raft. "But how am I going to talk to him if he's on the stage all night?" she added.

"He won't be. They never are."

But two hours and six cups of bug juice later, Jim was still on stage. The band was a hit, and everyone danced to their pared-down versions of oldies like "Brown-Eyed Girl" and "Good Lovin'." But even when his bandmates took a break, Jim stayed up there and played. In between conversations, Naomi stole glances at the stage, hoping to make eye contact or get a smile. But Jim was completely absorbed in his playing, his body and head arched around the guitar. He played jazz tunes without looking out at the audience as if he were practicing alone, his fingers moving rapidly over the frets.

As the dance was coming to an end, Naomi realized she had done almost no dancing; she'd just been sitting and listening to Jim play. She'd last seen Jennifer a half hour earlier, when her friend said she was going to the bathroom. Naomi decided to look for her, and was weaving in and out of dancing couples when the lifeguard Greg came up to her. "Psst,

Naomi," he whispered in her ear. "Tom and I have vodka in our cabin. C'mon!"

"Oh, alright. Let me just find Jennifer. Maybe we'll come over."

"Don't let us down."

After walking around the entire building, she darted quickly back to Jennifer's cabin, thinking maybe she had become tired or ill. But the cabin was quiet.

Returning to the social hall, Naomi wondered what she should do. Drinking cheap liquor with the boys sounded depressing. How had this night turned out to be such a disappointment? She'd been kidding herself, thinking that somehow Jim was going to sweep her off her feet.

Approaching the social hall from the back, she saw the silhouette of a couple sitting on the stone steps. Naomi considered finding another entrance to avoid interrupting this obviously romantic encounter, but she was already tired from wandering around; she just wanted to find Jennifer. She tiptoed up the steps, keeping her gaze up towards the light coming from the building.

"Naomi! It's you. I have barely seen you all evening," Mara said, turning her back for a moment on her companion. "Have you met Jim? He's the one responsible for the fab music we've had all night."

Naomi looked first at her sister, and then at the tall, lanky man beside her. He lifted his eyes to her. What was Mara doing with him?

"Yes. Yes I have," Naomi said. "Great music."

"Thanks. Better than my swimming I hope."

"So you two have already met," said Mara. "Jim here is going to be a great asset to camp this summer. We've been needing a better music program, and now we've got just the guy."

Mara moved a little closer to Jim on the step. Naomi was pretty sure she saw her sister's eyelashes flutter. How could she be flirting with him? He wasn't on the doctor track, was he? But she knew her sister well, and something was going on. Maybe it was the desperation of her approaching senior year making her latch on to any fresh meat that walked by.

"I was just heading to a little after-party at Greg and Tom's cabin," Naomi said. "Heard there might be something stronger than bug juice. Do you two want to join?"

"That sounds like just the thing," said Jim, standing up. "Figured someone must be having fun around these parts."

Looking at her feet, Mara picked up a small stone and rolled it around in her hand. Naomi knew she wouldn't come. As a member of the senior staff of the camp, Mara couldn't afford to be at a party with alcohol, even if she didn't take a sip. In truth, she was duty-bound to break it up, but Naomi knew she wouldn't, not wanting all the counselors to hate her. Also, even Mara wouldn't bust her own sister.

"I'm completely beat from all that dancing," Mara said. "It was really wonderful, but I've got to turn in now. We'll talk more tomorrow about the musical, Jim? Have a nice night." She gave them each a peck on the cheek and walked off.

Watching her sister disappear into the darkness of the softball field, Naomi felt a tinge of guilt. But she couldn't help also feeling happy with how things had worked out.

11

Reena

Reena lay low throughout Shabbat, staying out of the cabin and Allie's way. That morning at breakfast as they'd reached for the platter of coffee cake at the same time, Allie had practically bared her teeth and snarled. Reena wanted to ask Lila if it was true: if she had some kind of a claim on Ethan. But, then, when she imagined confronting her cousin, she got red-faced, because to even ask that question would be like admitting that she *wanted* to be with Ethan. And she didn't feel worthy of having that thought. She wasn't someone who guys noticed—especially not cute guys with long hair who play guitar and sing even when they're by themselves and think that no one is watching.

She sat on the beach on a towel through three consecutive free-swim periods, but didn't go in the water. Staring at the sky, clear blue with fast-moving clouds, she wondered: was this sky above her head the same as that above her father's on the opposite side of the globe? She imagined the Japanese sky as white and crisp. She imagined these cotton-ball clouds floating across that sky. She imagined she could catch a ride on a cloud, and float all the way to her father. She would surprise him—sneak up and congratulate him after one of his gigs.

She was still thinking about him when she sat up and looked around. Some younger kids were laughing and throwing sand at each other. A lifeguard said, "You do that one more time . . . !" The summer was half-over. Visiting Day, which marked the middle, was coming tomorrow. Not that anyone would be coming to visit *her*.

—

The next morning she sat on the spic-and-span cabin porch with the other girls, waiting. They'd been up until midnight cleaning, "until I can eat a sandwich right off the floor," said Susie, their counselor. Why the parents needed to be tricked into thinking that they were all obsessive-compulsive neat-freaks, Reena didn't understand.

The girls in the cabin were excited. A month earlier most of them were thrilled to get away; now they were like anxious kindergarteners waiting for their mommies and daddies.

All morning Reena had been feeling awkward, the way she always did when everyone made Mothers' Day cards at school. Visiting Day made clear exactly what she was missing.

Around ten in the morning, parents started walking up the dirt path from the meadow where they'd left their cars, laden with picnic baskets, coolers, lawn chairs, and blankets. Every square inch of playing fields, plus the boys' and girls' circles, was soon covered with families, eating and talking.

Reena had no choice; she was a guest of Aunt Mara and Uncle Gary. She let them kiss her on the cheek, and sat with them on their old plaid bed sheet under the maple tree outside the girls' cabins. Mara had brought cold-cut sandwiches in tin foil packages with names written on them: pastrami for Nathan and turkey for Lila. After weeks of eating macaroni, greasy grilled cheese, and sloppy Joes, the deli sandwiches were like an offering to prisoners: real food from the outside world.

"I had to guess for you, Reena," Mara said, handing her a turkey-on-rye.

"Thanks," Reena said, accepting it, though she would have preferred pastrami.

Reena had barely seen Nathan since they arrived,

as he spent most of his time on the opposite side of camp with the younger campers. He seemed changed —his skin was darker, he looked taller, less vulnerable. In between giant bites of sandwich, he talked non-stop about his friends, and how he helped design the scenery for his division's play, and the mural he'd been working on in arts and crafts.

"You have to come see it!" he said. "I drew all of the figures and now we're painting them and the art counselor said it's the best mural they've ever done. They might even hang it in the dining hall!"

"Yes, dear," said Mara. "Let's finish lunch and then you can take me to see it. I want to see your cabin, too."

"And I'd like to see that lake," said Gary. "Done any boating this summer?"

"My swim class is learning canoeing." Reena said.

Gary nodded, and Nathan cut in to talk about his friends' efforts to capsize a rowboat.

Reena had been looking forward to the overnight canoe trip that was coming up, but now she wasn't sure. Ethan would be there. She was afraid to even talk to him, for fear of what Lila would think. And what Allie would say.

Lila was quiet. She sat next to her mother, holding her hand. She seemed smaller and more fragile than she had all summer, as if she'd shrunk without her group of gabby girlfriends to prop her up.

Mara whispered something in Lila's ear. Lila nodded, and put her head in her mother's lap.

"Come on, let's go for a walk," Mara said, pulling Lila up to her feet. "Lila, why don't you take me to your activities, and Nathan can show Dad his?"

"Yes, good plan," said Gary. "Let's go."

Reena sat on the sheet, crumpling the tin foil in her hand, not sure what to do.

"You're welcome to join us," Mara said, looking down at her with her searching gaze. But Reena could tell from Lila's sour look that she wasn't wanted.

"I'll just hang out here."

"We'll be back later for dessert. I brought brownies."

"Brownies?" Nathan started to fumble through the cooler, but Gary grabbed the back of his shirt.

"Come on, buddy. Dessert can wait. Let's walk off the sandwiches first."

Reena was relieved that they'd all left; at least she wouldn't have to watch their bonding session anymore. But she felt self-conscious sitting by herself on their blanket. It felt wrong to be alone on Visiting Day. She stood up and wandered, thinking she might find Sharon, but she had no idea where she might be. She went to the bathroom and splashed cold water on her face. Even in the bathroom there were parents.

"Reena, this is my mom. Mom, this is Reena," said Margaret in an obligatory way. Her mother, exiting a toilet stall, smiled grandly.

"Nice to meetcha, Reena!"

"Hello," Reena said, hoping Margaret's mother wouldn't ask her how she liked camp, or where she came from, or what activities she and Margaret had together. *I've got to get out of here*, she thought. She slipped through the front door and walked across the haphazard quilt of picnic blankets that covered the girls' circle, carefully avoiding stepping on them by keeping to the seams.

As soon as she entered the path between the cabins Reena felt like she was a world away. The busy hum of the girls' circle was replaced by the sounds of crunching leaves under her feet as she made her way up to the place Ethan had called 'Blackberry Hill'. She reached the clearing and sat on the log.

She thought of the barefoot man, and the photograph of her mother with the person who looked like him. He couldn't possibly be the same man; he would have to have aged, and he didn't look old—his beard was blond, not gray.

Was she going mad? She thought of *Hamlet*, which her class had read that year in English; perhaps she had been visited by a spirit. But Hamlet's ghost is his dead father. If a ghost were to visit her, why would it be a strange man and not her own mother? He must not be a ghost.

The sun passed behind a cloud. *What am I doing here?* she thought. *Why did my father make me come here?*

12

Naomi

Naomi sat beside Jim on the slope of grass behind the boys' cabins, their legs stretched in front of them. It was a dark night with no moon, and Naomi had never seen so many stars.

"No view like this in Brooklyn." Jim leaned back on one elbow and sighed. "Never thought I'd be here right now."

"Where did you think you'd be, then?" Naomi passed him her old wool-covered canteen, half-full with a mixture of vodka and Coke. It had been her idea, after they'd been at Greg and Tom's party for a while, to fill the canteen and bring it here. At the party he'd been talking to everyone, and she wanted him to herself. She knew she might be getting in over her head; she didn't know the first thing about this guy.

"Painting houses, playing gigs. Let's just say it didn't work out. My dad showed me an ad in the Jewish News for this job. Seemed like a way to keep expenses flat and spend time in the woodshed."

"The woodshed?"

"You know, take your ax to the woodshed. It means practice. I thought if I went to some boring Jewish camp in the middle of nowhere I'd get time to practice guitar."

"Yeah, I know what you mean." Naomi was glad it was dark, because she cringed. *Some boring Jewish camp*. She might have described it the same way, but coming from his mouth it was as if he'd just criticized her family—only she was allowed to do that.

"It's great that you're so dedicated to your music. I wish I had that kind of dedication."

"What do you wish you were doing?"

"When I was younger I wanted to be an artist."

"And what happened?"

"At some point I realized I'm never going to be great. So I'm studying art history, instead." Naomi leaned back on the hill, and Jim turned to face her.

"Not sure I get it. Don't you still like to make art?"

"Yes." Naomi thought about how she had filled the pages of her sketchbook when she was at home before camp. She'd drawn the trees in the backyard, and the back of the house, and even, from memory, some city scenes.

"I say, do what you like. Don't worry about the competition. It'll kill anyone trying to be as good as the greats."

"But isn't that why you practice?"

"If I was trying to be Charlie Christian I'd have quit by now. The reason I practice is 'cause I want my guitar to make the sounds I hear in my head. And 'cause you need to do your time to even get in the game. And 'cause I like to play, damn it." He smiled.

Lying in the grass, Naomi nodded. "All good reasons. You want to know a secret?"

"If you want to tell one."

"I still draw, sometimes. I just don't show my drawings to anyone."

"So you're practicing, too."

"I guess."

They took sips from the canteen.

"Man, this is pretty great," Jim said.

"What is?"

"Lying here and looking at the stars. And meeting so many good people, like you and your sister. Already this summer is turning out to be different from what I expected."

Yes, Naomi thought. *For me, too*.

13

Reena

Reena found Sharon in her mother's cabin.

"Is Visiting Day the pits or what?" said Sharon.

"For you, too?"

"Yeah, it's the worst if you don't have someone visiting you. My grandparents sometimes come but this year they're on a cruise. Selfish, right?"

Reena laughed. "But your mom is here, and your dad comes up every weekend. You don't need visitors."

"False. I need them even more. Contact with the outside world. Proof that it still exists, etcetera."

"You can go hang out with Lila's parents, if you want," Reena said sarcastically.

"Your aunt and uncle? That's right, hey, why aren't you with them?"

"I was, I just don't feel like being around Lila."

"Yeah, I've noticed you and your cousin aren't exactly tight. What's up with that? Did you have a fight or something?"

"No, not really, we're just . . . different."

"But you're related," Sharon said.

"Yes, but we're nothing alike," Reena said. "It all started back when we were little kids, and we've never been close since then."

"What happened?" Sharon asked.

So Reena told her.

In the spring when they both turned eight, Lila came to visit Reena in the city.

Reena knew the whole thing had been at least partly orchestrated by their grandmother. Grandma had called one afternoon while Reena was doing her homework at the table inside the tiny kitchen. Her father was standing next to her, looking out the window above the sink with the phone to his ear.

"That's ridiculous," he said. "We always come for the holidays. Of course Reena knows her cousins."

Grandma spoke so loudly that Reena could make out some of what she was saying: "Jim, she needs her family. That's what Naomi would have wanted." Then there was silence on the other end, and she could imagine her grandmother furrowing her brow.

"If you're implying that I'm deliberately keeping Reena away from Mara and Gary's kids, you've got it wrong. You know as well as me it's not that simple."

Her father turned around and caught Reena looking at him. He winked.

"Sorry, Nancy, got to go. Reena needs help with her homework. Bye." He hung up and pulled down a pot off the rack to start making dinner. "So, do you need any help with your homework?"

"No," Reena said.

"Let me know if you do."

When Lila called later, Reena knew it was because Grandma had put her up to it. But that didn't stop her from inviting her cousin for a sleepover. She wanted to be better friends with her cousin. Besides, though she'd been to her house in New Jersey many times, Lila had never once come to see where Reena lived.

She and her father lived in a one-bedroom in Stuyvesant Town, a giant complex of identical red-brick apartment buildings just north of the East Village. They moved there about a year after her mother died, which meant it was the only home she could remember. Stuy Town was no-frills, but Reena loved it. In between the buildings there were grass and playgrounds and athletic courts. It was the kind of place where you knew lots of people by face and it was okay to smile at them.

On the Friday of the sleepover, Aunt Mara drove Lila into the city. Reena and her father waited for them on the street, so that Mara wouldn't have to find a parking spot. Reena jumped rope on the corner of First and Sixteenth for what seemed like hours, while her dad paced nearby, checking his phone. When the navy Buick finally pulled up, Lila tumbled out the back. Her dark curly hair was pulled back in a ponytail and her skin was pale.

Aunt Mara rolled down the window. "Traffic from you-know-where! Poor Lila's been sick. Keep her out in the fresh air for a while okay? Have a great time, girls. *Shabbat Shalom*!" She barely looked at Reena's father. Then she sped away.

"You should live in the city," Reena told her green cousin. "We never ride in cars."

The first place Reena took Lila was to her favorite playground. It had a jungle gym, three backless swings and a couple of little playhouses. She'd been playing there since she'd learned to walk. She tried to get Lila to play hide-and-seek, then tag, but her cousin wasn't interested. They went on the swings for a while until some other kids turned up and they all started playing King of the Mountain, which meant climbing to the top of the jungle gym and trying to keep invaders off your turf. Lila didn't play for long. Reena found her sitting on a bench kicking her feet.

"Do you know those kids?" she asked.

"Sure. I've seen them around."

"What are their names?"

Reena thought about this for a moment, trying to remember what she'd heard them calling each other. "One is Jane, and I think her sister is Caroline. Not sure about the others."

"Don't you ever get tired of playing with strangers?"

"They're not strangers!" Reena said. "They're kids from the neighborhood. They live here, like me."

Lila nodded, but Reena didn't think she understood.

On Saturday morning they went to the jazz brunch at Park Avalon, where you could get French toast filled with sweet mascarpone and cherries, and Reena's father's friend Bob played upright bass with his group every week. Sometimes her father would sit in, and that day he'd brought his guitar. After two cups of coffee and one mimosa, he went up and played "My Favorite Things." Reena felt her chest swell; she knew he was playing it for her.

They were full of sweet breakfast and hot chocolate, and her father had slapped all the musicians' hands, and they were on their way out through the giant swinging glass doors, when Lila said she had a bellyache. Then she added, "I think it would've been better with a singer, don't you?" "I loved it," Reena said. But as soon as it came out she felt silly. Maybe she wasn't supposed to like her father's music.

In the afternoon they went to the Temple of Dendur at the Met, one of Reena and her father's favorite places. He said that standing beneath those giant old stones, you could almost feel the warm breeze coming off the Nile; but at the same time, all you had to do was look out the window and you knew you were in Central Park. Since forever, they would go there and pretend they were ancient Egyptians. The game had started with a story he'd told her about her mother: once when Reena was a baby, they'd stood together beside the transplanted Egyptian temple, and she'd declared that she was an ancient queen, and her baby a princess.

—

Hoping to introduce Lila to their game, Reena touched her shoulders with a pretend scepter. "Princess Lila," she said, "Behold, I grant to you the riches of this mighty land."

"You're so weird, Reena," Lila said. "And these mummies are creepy! Can we go?"

Dad looked at Reena and shrugged.

When Lila insisted on stopping in the gift shop, he bought each girl a postcard. On the way out he whispered to Reena, "At least she can tell Mara that we took her to temple."

Reena slipped her hand in her father's. She was beginning to think that inviting Lila to the city had been a big mistake.

Still, she and Lila bonded in their own way. They tried on each other's clothes and dragged a chair into the tiny black-and-white bathroom so they could take turns climbing up and looking at themselves in the mirror above the sink. Reena felt ridiculous in Lila's girly-girl heart-covered dress, and Lila looked equally uncomfortable in Reena's favorite skull t-shirt and cowgirl boots. But neither could deny that the sizes were perfect.

Lila taught Reena how to do elaborate clapping games that she played with her friends at school. Soon she had all of these nonsensical rhythmic chants running through her head all the time: "Bo, bo, skee wattin-tottin, a-a, a-a, boom, boom, boom." Her father said it sounded like scatting.

But they didn't stay up late talking, like Reena did with her friends when they slept over. Lila brushed her teeth, went to the bathroom, got into Reena's bed, and fell asleep. Reena lay wide-awake in a sleeping bag on the floor, listening to the rhythmic ebb and flow of her cousin's breathing. She went outside to the living room, where her father was watching a philharmonic concert on Channel 13. Eventually she fell asleep next to him on the sofa, which doubled as his bed.

In the morning, Reena told Lila they were like the city mouse and the country mouse.

Lila said, "That's ridiculous, I'm from Fallwood, New Jersey. That's not the country!"

But then, they went out to get bagels and a homeless drunk who was always pacing on First Avenue started shouting maniacally. Lila grabbed Reena's hand and nearly pushed her into the traffic to get away from him. She looked terrified.

"Don't worry. He doesn't bite," Reena said.

Lila did not appear comforted. When they returned to the apartment, she called her parents and said she was ready to leave and could they please come now?

Uncle Gary came to get her and once again they met the car on the street. Dad and Reena both gave Lila kisses and told her to come again, though they knew that she wouldn't.

—

"Even though we're cousins, we're not really friends. Does that make sense?" Reena said. She thought now, too, about the *afikoman* incident on Passover, and how Lila had left her alone to take the heat.

"Yes," Sharon said. "Do you think it will always be that way?"

"I don't know."

14

Naomi

Out on the deep raft during free swim, Naomi got lost in her thoughts. She'd settled into a routine of teaching swimming and lifeguarding, and found that time sped by while she critiqued strokes, reminding kids to lift their elbows and kick under the water. Guarding free swim was dull, though. She got bored and nervous standing out there watching daredevil kids hold their breath under the black surface of the lake. She hated reinforcing the rules; sometimes she felt like a cop, blowing her whistle when a camper swam outside of the swim area, hissing at another to shut up during roll call.

She softened when she saw Jim come down the steps for his daily swim. He was there, he claimed, for the exercise, but she hoped that maybe he was keeping up the regular routine in order to see her, too. He winked at her before he jumped in, and then she watched his every stroke for thirty minutes.

She smiled, remembering their walk in the darkness together on the night of the dance. They had started something that night, but what exactly she didn't know. She hadn't seen him much since, since they were both busy working. Once she'd passed him and Mara, walking and talking, and he'd winked then, too. He was a winker! Which was weird and old-fashioned. But she liked his attention, and she didn't like Mara having it instead of her.

"Are you okay?" Mara had asked Naomi, the morning after the dance, at breakfast.

"Of course, why?"

"Because some of the counselors were in bad

shape last night. Stephanie Markowitz threw up right in front of B-2. There are formal warnings going out today, through every division head."

"Thanks for the heads up, I guess, although I do feel just a little accused."

"I'm just letting you know. Once the campers arrive, any staff member caught with drinks or drugs will be sent home. I wouldn't want it to be you."

Naomi felt sure that Mara's warning was something of a threat. Maybe it was really about Jim. Leave it to the Gordon girls to be interested in the same new staff member.

When Jim finished his laps, he swam up to Naomi's raft.

"Been doing any drawing?" he asked.

"Yes, in fact," she said, without taking her eyes off the swimming children.

"Good. 'Cause I don't wanna be the only one practicing all the time."

She smiled. "Sorry, can't talk right now. I'm guarding."

"Ok, don't want to distract the lifeguard. See you later, Nay." Her heart pounded for a few moments after he left. He'd given her a nickname.

15

Reena

A pall fell over the cabin after Visiting Day. It all started when Allie, in a foul mood, accused everyone, including her friends, of having used up her expensive Kiehl's conditioner. "It's Michael's fault," Allie said in a breathy, angry voice. "I gave it to her, and she left it in the shower, and all of you just helped yourselves. Cretins." The girls, in a frenzy of denial, were whispering and scheming and vying to be allowed to comfort Allie, who was acting like she'd had a death in the family.

Reena and Sharon sat together on the top bunk, trying not to be heard. "Why'd she leave her precious conditioner in the shower if it was so irreplaceable?" Reena whispered.

"Who cares?" Sharon said. "I'm so sick of Allie and all her drama. Look at Michael. She's crying in her pillow and no one even gives a shit. They're all trying to make Allie happy. I think we're living with a bunch of zombies."

"What did you say?" Allie piped up. "You know we can all hear you."

"Nothing," Reena said.

"No, not 'nothing,' Lila's cousin. You sit there calling us names, and you think you can get away with it? Wait, maybe it was *you* who used my conditioner."

"No, I didn't," Reena said. "And, I have a name."

"Well, so do I, and it was written on my bottle of Kiehl's. Did you not see it when you helped yourself?"

"She didn't use your conditioner, Allie!" Sharon said.

"Oh, no? How do you know? Have you two been showering together again?"

"Disgusting," said someone, down below.

"Lila, is your cousin a thief?" Allie asked.

Lila, who had been one of the whisperers on Allie's bed, shrugged her shoulders.

"Everyone watch out," Allie said. "There are thieves in this cabin. You never know who might be after your stuff."

"How are we going to survive this?" Reena whispered in Sharon's ear.

"It will blow over," Sharon whispered back. "They're all just homesick but they won't admit it. Happens every year after Visiting Day. You're lucky. At least you get to escape. I wish *I* was going on the canoe trip."

—

It was already hot at six in the morning when the members of Reena's swim group started packing up the minivan for the canoe trip. They met down at the lake, where they grabbed the life jackets and paddles. They had taken out the metal canoes a handful of times in preparation for the trip, when Ellen had invited Dave to guest-teach the class. Dave was a waterfront staff member who looked like a marine— short and stocky with a crew cut. He taught them the J-stroke, the draw stroke, and how to get back in a capsized canoe. He taught them to lean on their knees on the hard metal floor, rather than sit on the seats. Now it was time to see if they could hack it in the wilderness: they were setting off on a two-day trip down the Housatonic River, with a night of camping in between.

"Ready for an adventure?" Ellen turned around and asked, as the van bounced out of camp, dragging the canoe trailer.

"You guys need to decide on partners," Dave said from the driver's seat. "Canoeing is all about partnership and you're going to be working together for the next two days."

There were only six of them, and at least one pairing was clear: Sam and Jeff were always together, and had won the Visiting Day regatta as sailing partners. They were sitting in the back seat, passing comic books back and forth. Reena looked at the back of Ethan's head, wondering if he might turn around and ask her—but then Gail tapped her knee and asked, "Partner?"

At first Reena was surprised that Gail asked her and not Michael, but then she understood. With arms crossed and a frown on her face, Michael obviously was not excited about the trip. You'd think Michael would be happy to get away from Allie. Reena certainly was. But who knows what was going on in Michael's head. Reena had to say yes to Gail. Besides, Ethan hadn't asked her. Still looking at his back, she replied, "Sure."

They arrived at the riverbank and carried the canoes to the water's edge. By the time they loaded them up and pushed off, it was almost ten, and the sun was scorching. Reena splashed water on her face to cool off, and it turned instantly to beads of sweat. She pulled her floppy sunhat firmly onto her head and then carefully steered the canoe away from the bank. She was in the back, steering. Gail was the power paddler, and turned out to be a great partner, because she was strong. Reena followed her partner's lead: when Gail switched to the left side, she switched to the right, and so on. But the river was low and moving very slowly, so the paddling was hard. Sometimes Gail would just stop and rest, and Reena would stick her paddle in the water like a rudder, trying to keep the canoe going straight.

Reena liked being on the river. It was exciting and different to be out of camp, and she loved the sense that they were covering mileage—getting somewhere, unlike the usual boating in circles on the lake. The scenery was constantly changing, as they passed under rickety wooden bridges, and by charming villages with red painted houses and white church steeples. In between there were long stretches where all they could see were forests of tall pine trees. There were places where the water ran faster, and where they had to watch out for obstacles. "V!" Gail shouted, which meant there was a rock ahead and they had to steer around it. Sam and Jeff were beached in the middle of the river at one point, their canoe spinning round and round. Reena and Gail pulled over to the side of the river and ate handfuls of trail mix while Dave and Ellen pushed the boys' canoe off. Then they took turns jumping in the water to cool down.

They were a little pack of four canoes: Sam and Jeff in the lead, then Reena and Gail, then Michael and Ethan, and the counselors in the rear. Michael and Ethan were having problems. They kept lagging way behind, and Reena heard Ethan complain, "but she's hardly paddling!" Every time she heard them arguing, Reena couldn't help feeling secretly glad. She didn't want Ethan to have fun with Michael.

By late afternoon, Reena's shoulders and back were aching from all the paddling, and she'd lost the feeling in her knees and thighs. She thought of her father, who was always rolling his head around, trying to loosen a kink in his neck. For the first time, she understood what a sore neck felt like.

Dave told them to link canoes for a pow-wow, so they lined up the boats beside each other like the pieces of a picket fence. "We're approaching the campground," he said. "We'll take the lead here, so don't go ahead of us. I don't want anyone missing the exit, so to speak, and it comes up quick. Look for a small beach on the left, just after the big boulder in the center of the river."

Gail and Reena landed right behind Mike and Ellen. Reena had never felt such relief at the end of a day. She got out of the canoe and jumped up and down, just to feel her feet touch the ground.

The campsite was a couple hundred feet up from the riverbank. They took their things out of the canoes, and pushed the boats over beside each other for the night. Then they changed into dry clothes and set up two tents, one for girls and one for boys. Dave was cooking pasta on a kerosene stove, and he asked volunteers to search for kindling for the campfire.

"I'll go," Ethan said.

"So will I," Reena said. She wanted to talk to Ethan again. Lila and Allie weren't there watching, so she figured it would be okay. They crunched through the trees, and went further away than they needed to. The woods seemed to go on forever. Reena kept thinking that they'd hit a trail, like in Central Park, but they didn't.

"Do you know the way back?" she asked.

"Not sure, actually," he said. He spun around in circles. "Let's ask our wildlife friends," he joked, using his hands to imitate the call of an owl.

"Seriously!" She laughed, maybe too loudly. He wasn't *that* funny. But she couldn't help smiling around him. "Follow me," she said, and he did. She walked in the direction that she thought was right and then stopped abruptly, to listen for the sound of their group at the campsite. Ethan bumped right into her, his armful of twigs falling to the ground.

"Sorry," he said, and put a hand on her back as he leaned down to pick them up. Reena felt heat rise up her spine. She had never felt anything like that before. She crouched down beside him, and helped him pick up the twigs. Their heads were almost touching, and when Ethan looked up, Reena found herself looking right into his eyes.

"Thanks," he said, and looked away.

She felt overcome by shyness. She almost couldn't remember how to talk. They didn't say anything else, and he didn't look at her again, as they reversed their footsteps and found their way back to the campsite, dumping their armfuls of twigs by the fire pit.

Later, they all sat on logs around the campfire holding metal mugs of "Russian tea"—a mixture of Tang and powdered iced-tea stirred into boiling water. It tasted surprisingly good. Ellen sang campfire songs in her cracking muppet voice, and everyone joined in. Even Michael, who'd spent more time scowling than laughing in her canoe, sang along to "American Pie." She seemed to have softened since they'd arrived at the campsite. She was probably relieved, as Reena had been, to find clean flushing toilets, despite rumors all day that they'd have to dig holes. Everyone was a little giddy—they'd made it down the river, and tonight they'd sleep in tents under the stars.

Eventually the fire collapsed to embers, and one by one the adventurers crawled into their tents to go to sleep. But Reena wasn't tired; she was still feeling tingly, and wanted to stay outside with Ethan, looking at the stars. There were so many they looked like snowflakes in a storm. She felt like she could stay up forever. Reena started humming and when she looked at Ethan, he joined in. Behind the sound of their voices was the rushing of the river. When they finished singing there was no one left around the dying fire but them. She was conscious of acting against her own nature. She was shy, and weak-kneed. Wasn't she? She smiled at Ethan, and beckoned him to come closer.

It was getting cold out, and she felt goose bumps on her legs. Or was it simply nerves? She didn't know what Ethan thought about her. The not knowing was the scariest thing.

"What should we sing next?" she said. She felt his leg against hers.

"Let's just listen."

She could hear the crackle of the fire embers, the rushing river, and the chirping of night insects. But her heart, skipping beats, sounded loudest of all.

"I can't believe I didn't know you—or anyone here—just a few weeks ago," she said. "That's strange isn't it?"

"You knew Lila."

"I thought I knew her, but now I'm not sure. You may have noticed we're not exactly besties."

"Just because you're in the same family, doesn't mean you have to be best friends," he said. "My dad doesn't talk to his brother anymore. They had a fight like ten years ago, and they just gave up." "But it still kinda sucks," she said. "Especially if you don't have a lot of family to begin with."

"Yeah, you're right. I've tried to ask my dad what happened but he won't talk about it." Ethan pushed his hair out of his eyes with one hand, and dug a stick into the dirt at his feet with the other. They both stared at the remains of the fire.

"So what about Lila?" Reena asked.

"What about her?"

"I heard you were, like, going out with her?"

"People say stupid things," he said.

"But Allie told me . . ."

"I could kill that girl. She thinks she's a goddess or something. Last summer Allie got some notion that she wanted to couple up all of her friends, so she convinced a bunch of guys to ask them out. I took Lila to the square dance. Big deal. And anyway, Lila barely talked to me. As soon as the dancing was over she ran back to her friends."

Reena was relieved to hear him say all this, but she also felt pity for her cousin. Why couldn't Lila see through Allie's bullshit?

"Allie accused me of stealing you away from Lila," Reena said. She felt her face get hot.

Ethan took her hand, and she felt that warm current go down her spine again. Could he feel the way she was shaking? "Allie's got a big head," he said. "And she doesn't have a clue about me."

They walked down to the water, past the pile of overturned canoes. It was brighter there, with no trees to block the view of the lit-up night sky. Ethan held her hand the whole time, and she couldn't stop shaking.

"I can't believe I'm here," she said, as they stood just at the river's edge.

"What do you mean?"

"I mean, I didn't even want to come to camp this summer. It was some crazy idea of my dad's. It's been hard."

"Everybody misses home when they're at camp. Even if they don't say so."

"It's just all very new," Reena said. "I've never spent more than a week outside the city. I've never slept in the woods before. I've never seen stars like this. I've never canoed down a river."

"Have you ever done this?" He turned and brushed his lips gently against hers.

She smiled. Reena had kissed boys before, but those times were little more than dares—quick pecks to show that they could. This was different. Like the wilderness where they stood, kissing Ethan was more vivid and alive than she could have imagined. It was a very good kind of new.

—

Reena woke up on the floor of the tent, rocks in her back, still smiling. She wasn't sure how it would be that morning, with Ethan. So she was happy when he stood beside her during *t'filot*. The group gathered, just after waking up, by the riverside, and murmured the prayers to themselves using small soft-covered *siddurs*. "Praised are You, Lord our God, King of the universe who creates the heavens and the earth/ who provides for all our needs/ who guides us on our path," Reena read. But as this was silent, personal prayer, she could pray for anything she wanted. She thought of her father, and hoped he was well, and imagined him also thinking of her right at this moment. She thought of her mother, all the unanswered questions swirling around her memory, and hoped that she would find answers one day. Standing beside Ethan, the morning sun flickering on their faces, Reena felt gratitude for the kiss. *Thank you, God, for this canoe trip, and for bringing me to this place with this person on this day.*

After twenty minutes of standing and swaying beside each other in silence, they sang "*Adon Olam*" together, in a tune Reena knew already, after just several weeks, as well as any record in her dad's collection. As they were singing, she thought she heard a familiar voice, sweet and lilting, coming from behind them. She turned around, but saw only the thickness of the woods, trees rustling in the morning breeze.

16

Naomi

As she turned off the shower after a long day down by the lake, Naomi heard the faint sound of a guitar coming from the woods behind her cabin. The circle of girls' bunks was quiet, as the campers were at dinner. She stood by the window and listened. Jim practiced as much as he'd claimed–she'd seen him hunched over his guitar on the porch of his cabin, ten-year-old boys running in and out and slamming doors, and baseballs whizzing past. But she was surprised to hear him playing by the girls' cabins.

She slipped into a sundress and sandals, tied her hair back, and stepped outside. Following the sound of the guitar, she wove between two cabins and entered a path that led up to the clearing where they used to make campfires when she was a camper. The clearing was no longer maintained and had become smaller as the brush had grown in over the years. Now the only time anyone ventured up there was to pick blackberries—at the beginning of August, the bushes around the clearing exploded with the sweet, wild fruit. As she continued up the path, Naomi remembered the summer—she might have been eleven or twelve—when she had become ill from eating too many berries. It was too much to bear knowing that the fruit would only last a week or two, after which it would shrivel and sour or be eaten by worms and birds. Having no place to store or can the blackberries, there'd been no choice but to swallow as many as possible. They were, as she recalled, sublimely delicious.

Jim must have tired of practicing with all the mayhem on the front porch of his cabin. She wondered who had told him about Blackberry Hill, and if he'd mind being interrupted. Maybe he'd be pleased to see her, as she hoped.

Pausing for a moment to quiet the crunching of leaves and twigs under her feet, Naomi listened just outside the clearing for the sound of the guitar. But now she couldn't hear the twangy sound of strings; instead, she heard someone humming. She entered the clearing.

Naomi felt her mouth fall open, like a goofball on *Candid Camera*. Could this really be happening? It wasn't Jim, and there was no guitar. Standing in front of her was the weird guy from Washington Square Park. Humming what sounded like an old Hassidic tune, he had his back turned to her, and was looking at the bushes, maybe searching for berries. He had an entrancing voice, and Naomi stood frozen, listening. The melody was similar to one her grandmother used to sing to her—a little piece of the old country. She hummed along in recognition, and he turned around.

"Welcome!" he said, smiling broadly.

"What are you doing here?" Naomi asked. There was no logical reason that she could come up with why he would be standing on Blackberry Hill. Had he somehow followed her to camp? It was impossible.

"Delivering God's message of truth and love."

Maybe he's come for *tzedakah*, she reasoned. The camp was known for social-action projects with the surrounding community; maybe this poor *shlub* had heard that he'd get a kosher hand-out.

"Do you need help with something?" she asked, trying to keep her mind open.

"You are kind to God's emissary. You shall be rewarded."

God's emissary? What, like an angel? Deep breath.

"God will show you the way," he said, and began humming again. "Proceed at his will." He started to leave the clearing.

She had never met anyone so odd: he must be on some crazy trip. And yet she'd wondered so much about him since their first meeting that she couldn't just let him go.

"Wait," said Naomi. "How will I know when I've found love?"

"Sing with me," he said. He sang, building his wordless tune slowly, louder and louder. So she sang along, following his notes and rhythm. And when he started dancing, crossing and uncrossing his feet as he circled around the clearing, she too began to dance.

They danced and danced, and Naomi forgot that she was in camp. She forgot that the man beside her was a nut from New York who couldn't logically be upstate with her in the woods. She forgot that she was a bit lost herself, unsure how to connect the dots between the little girl she once was, and the woman she was becoming. While singing and dancing, she felt satisfied and happy, the way she'd felt after the second cup of blackberries that summer she was twelve, but before the third.

"Follow your heart to God and love will find you," he said, still dancing. And then he danced down the path and away, leaving Naomi in a dissipating cloud of ecstasy. She wondered if love felt anything like this.

17

Reena

Reena returned to her cabin from the canoe trip in the evening, dirty, damp and exhausted. The second day on the river had ended with them all getting caught in a downpour. She was looking forward to telling Sharon everything, but Sharon wasn't there, so she dropped her things by her bed, and started getting ready to shower.

"So you and Ethan have fun on the wild river?" Allie said. Reena turned around. Michael was standing by Allie's side, so Reena knew where her information had come from. Michael had found a way to get back under Allie's wing, after the conditioner incident. Reena thought that she and Michael had bonded a little that day, huddled together under a plastic tarp waiting out the rain. Maybe she was wrong.

"None of your business," Reena said, heading to the bathroom.

But Allie blocked her way. "Oh, you're right. It's not. But it's your cousin's business. Did you ask her if she cared?"

Reena had been thinking about that, a lot, since the night before. Allie was right; she *should* talk to Lila. About anything! Forget Ethan, they never talked to each other *at all*.

Reena walked over to Lila's bed, where she was lying on her side, facing the wall. "Lila, we need to talk."

"I'm tired." Lila answered without turning around.

"Well, wake up." Reena could feel the eyes of a gathering circle of girls on her back. "I need to talk to you. Now."

Lila rolled over and looked beyond Reena into the center of cabin. Reena knew she was looking for Allie to save her, so she stepped closer to her, blocking her cousin's view. *Look at me!* she wanted to shout. *Stop ignoring me and wake up and talk to me! This is not about Allie; this is about us!* Slowly, Lila's eyes lifted to meet Reena's, and she stood up. Reena put her hand on Lila's shoulder and led her towards the door, and the girls in the cabin parted ways to let them out. They sat down on the porch steps, staring straight ahead into the darkness. Reena could hear yelps and shrieks from the surrounding cabins, as the girls inside got ready for bed.

"What do you want?" Lila said, folding her arms over her knees and letting her head rest on them.

Lila seemed so sad that Reena wondered if this was the right time to confront her. What was wrong with her? Wasn't this *her* camp, where she had all of her closest friends?

"Are you okay?" Reena asked.

Lila just shrugged her shoulders. Reena decided to press on.

"Allie needs to leave me alone. She's constantly on my case."

"What do you want me to do?"

Reena took a deep breath. "This isn't really about Ethan, is it? Because he said there's nothing between him and you." Reena felt bad spilling it out like that, admitting that they'd been speaking about her.

"I used to like Ethan, like, last summer. I thought he might like me, too. But I don't know. I want him to."

"Oh," Reena said. Did that mean she shouldn't have kissed him? What did she owe Lila, anyway?

"So is that why Allie's the way she is, towards me?"

"Allie doesn't like you," Lila said.

"No kidding! But why? What did you tell her about me?"

"I didn't say anything, I swear. Allie just gets these ideas. From the first week she had it out for you, maybe because you were friends with Sharon."

"Well, thanks for sticking up for me, Cuz."

Lila looked at her. "What do you want me to do? Allie can be kind of crazy. She wouldn't talk to me yesterday because she blamed me for spilling bug juice on her white Toms. But it wasn't my fault! She was the one who was running in the dining hall and tripped and fell right into me. And then she kept saying that I bumped into *her*, which I didn't even do. I can't control her!"

"OK, fine, forget about Allie. I don't care about her." Reena wanted to say*: I care about you. You're my cousin.* But she couldn't say it, because Lila didn't seem to care about her, and because she wasn't sure it was true. They sat in silence for a minute or two. Lila stared straight ahead into the dark. Reena could hear the girls in the bunk shuffling around, probably trying to hear what they were saying. "But I still don't understand why, this whole summer, you've been so cold—"

Lila cut her off. "There's not a day that's gone by in my whole life when my mother hasn't mentioned you and Aunt Naomi. Not *one* day. You think I don't know the way your dad kept you from us all these years?"

"That's not true," Reena said, but she felt a pit open in her stomach. She had always noticed that her father avoided Aunt Mara. But she had assumed it was mutual. She thought Mara didn't want to see him, either. Could she have been wrong?

"And it seems to me you're just like him," Lila continued. "Standing off to the side, whispering with Sharon, disappearing by yourself all the time. Who's the cold one? And now you want me to help you? It's like you think you're better. But just because your mom died doesn't make you better."

Lila stood up and went back into the cabin, letting the door thwack shut. Reena sat on the steps wiping tears away with the backs of her hands.

18

Naomi

Naomi could not believe what was happening to her. She was preoccupied, unexpectedly, with two men. One who was flesh and blood but remained out of arm's reach; and the other seemingly not of this world. Camp, this place she knew as well as the outline of her mother's face, had become completely unfamiliar; a place where she never knew what to expect next.

She found herself going up to Blackberry Hill more frequently, wondering if the man—if he was a man—might show up again. One afternoon when she finished at the lake for the day, she brought her sketchbook up into the clearing. She used colored pencils to draw the dense barbed bushes, and a patch of pink wildflowers — humming his tune as she worked. When the long shadows of late afternoon appeared, she realized she was probably missing dinner. It was time to go. As she stood up from her crossed-legged position on the ground, her feet went numb with pins and needles; she yelped in pain as she hopped down the path into the girls' circle.

Mara was there to greet her, clutching a clipboard to her chest and wearing a funny fretful look on her face. Instinctively, Naomi hid her sketchbook and pencils behind her back.

"What were you doing up there?" Mara asked, pointing to the path.

"Why do you ask?"

"Just wondering, is all."

"You don't need to sound so suspicious. What's the big deal about going up Blackberry Hill? I like it there."

Mara stepped closer, and brought her voice down, speaking into Naomi's ear. "I heard something just now, as I was walking by. Now, I've heard what people have been saying about you but I didn't believe it."

"Believe what?" Naomi felt her cheeks flush. "Who's been saying what about me?"

"People have heard noises coming down from the hill, and they've seen you coming and going, and the word is that you're having some kind of a . . . a . . . tryst up there."

Naomi looked at Mara, her face serious and concerned, and started laughing. "Oh, is that what they're saying? And with whom, pray tell, are they saying I'm trysting?"

Mara looked down at her sandaled feet. "Well I don't know. Who were you up there with? If you're going with someone, you don't need to keep it a secret, you know."

"Oh, Mara. You and your rumor mill. You want to know who I was up there with? Ok, I'll tell you. He's a magical mystery man, with a beautiful voice and a beard and a thing for religious sayings. But don't be expecting an introduction. Sorry. He's hard to pin down."

"What are you talking about? Naomi, are you okay?"

"Oh, yes, I'm fine. Just fine." Naomi laughed again. "But I wouldn't trust your sources anymore. Things are almost never what they say. See you later, Sis." She went back to her cabin to put her art supplies away and to try to catch the end of dinner.

19

Reena

Reena needed Sharon more than ever, but for the next day her only friend was hardly around. Sharon was physically there at meals and at bedtime, but she was acting so strange: whispering with Lila of all people, and missing out on activities. With the girls in the cabin following Allie's lead, and Lila mad at her, Reena was starting to feel invisible.

Then the whole camp was sent to the basketball courts for the evening program. It was unusual for all the divisions to be together, and there was murmuring on all sides about what it could mean. Reena saw Ethan standing with his cabin-mates. He looked at her, raising an eyebrow. She looked away, nervous. That feeling, the heat in her spine, was something she wanted again, but also feared. Reena worried that she'd dreamt up everything that had happened on the canoe trip. She'd seen Ethan since, but at places like the lake or in the art studio, when he was with his group of friends, and then he hadn't done or said anything to indicate that their relationship had changed. She wasn't about to go beg him to hang out with her.

Besides, whether or not she had a right to be, Reena knew that Lila *was* jealous. She didn't want to share any of her friends with Reena, girls or boys. Reena was afraid she'd broken some unspoken rule from the camp etiquette handbook, a book that, if it existed, would be written in a tongue that she didn't speak. Maybe she was better off pretending that nothing had ever happened between her and Ethan.

Reena certainly didn't need any more reasons for

her cousin to be angry with her. She couldn't stop thinking about Lila's accusations the night before on the porch. She wondered if something had happened to cause the rift between her dad and Mara, if there really was a rift. Lila was dead wrong about *her*; that she knew. Reena didn't think she was better because she had lost her mom. She thought she was forever missing something, something that Lila had with Mara and that she could only ever observe from the outside.

The crowd erupted in applause when two groups of campers ran onto center-court carrying banners. There was Sharon, wearing white shorts and t-shirt, surrounded by other white-clad kids. On the other side of the court stood a group wearing all blue; Lila was among them.

"What's going on?" Reena asked.

"Color War break out!" someone answered.

The camp director, Rabbi Warren, approached the microphone. He was a short man with a receding hairline and a belly. "Welcome to Color War!" he roared.

The crowd roared back.

"Introducing your team captains!" said Rabbi Warren. Each division had a boy and girl captain for each team. Lila and Sharon each got their turn in the spotlight as they were introduced.

Minutes later the bunk counselors read out the team assignments. Reena was on Blue: Lila's team, not Sharon's. The whole camp was split down the middle, Blue versus White, and would spend the next twenty-four hours engaged in constant battle for points: points for the winner of each sporting event, points for keeping quiet during meals, points for learning the team's cheers, etc.

Reena hated team sports. She had so far made it through the daily period of sports at camp by choosing games that didn't involve competitive teammates yelling "Pass!" or "Score!" No soccer, basketball, nor the dreaded volleyball if she could avoid it; archery and yoga were the athletic activities for her.

She headed across camp with the rest of the Blue team to the Social Hall, where they would learn their team's songs and cheers. Lila stood at the front with the other captains, looking nervously pleased. Why had *she* been chosen to be a captain?

Reena had so many questions about Color War, and it was so frustrating to not be able to ask them of her usual camp guide, Sharon. But Sharon was too busy roaming the grounds with the other White captains, rooting and cheering. She seemed very happy in her new role of importance, encouraging the camper peons to "give it your best!" Between the days of secret meetings and all the attention from the older captains and counselors, her head was turning into an overinflated balloon that Reena thought might float away.

The next day, Susie woke up the cabin early and instructed everyone to wear their team color. Reena wore her turquoise Mardi Gras t-shirt and a pair of cut-offs. Trying to get into the spirit, she tied her curls back with a blue rubber band. No one could say she wasn't trying.

The first game was volleyball. Reena stood in the back of the court and tried her best to get out of the way so that the better players could get the ball. Her teammates, needless to say, were not always appreciative of her strategy.

"For God's sake, Reena, that ball was coming straight at you!" said Lila, exasperated, after the ball dropped like a dead bird on the asphalt beside her.

"Sorry," Reena said. She was a handicap, and she knew it.

Allie, on the White team, stood right in front of the net, and took every opportunity to jump up and pound the ball with the back of her fist. Each time she scored a point, she cackled with glee. This put Sharon in a difficult position; her arch-enemy was also her greatest advantage. Sharon was playing back-court like Reena, and was more cheerleader than key player. Each time her team scored, be it through Allie's aggressiveness or any other means, Sharon hooted. She wanted to win.

In the second half, the counselors refereeing the game insisted that everyone switch positions. Reena moved up to the net and concentrated on the ball, trying to picture what she would do if it actually came near her. Lila lobbed a serve straight to Allie, almost as if they were working together, and Allie spiked it hard. The ball was coming at Reena. She froze. She didn't even lift her arms. She just stood there as it smacked her in the face.

She trudged off to the infirmary cupping her hands to her face, blood from her nose dripping through her fingers. She wasn't sure what upset her most—the pain, the embarrassment, or the realization that her Mardi Gras t-shirt was ruined.

The last words she heard as she left the court were Lila's: "We're better off without her."

Her face was hot from shame, and fury. Her cousin, the only person in camp who shared her blood, couldn't care less about her. At least the facts were confirmed.

Reena sat out the next several activities. The flow of blood stopped relatively quickly, but the insult lasted. She sat on the sidelines of a basketball game, watching Sharon and Lila cheer their hearts out. Neither one asked how she was feeling. If they had, she wouldn't have told them the truth anyway. She wouldn't have said that she thought Allie Berger had an aggressive personality disorder and should be sent to military camp. She wouldn't have said that she felt lonely and abandoned.

—

Late in the afternoon, it came out that the two teams were neck-and-neck, with only a few activities left in the day. Next was swimming.

Back in the cabin, the girls changed into their swimsuits. Reena sat on her bed and finished a lanyard she'd been working on, weaving the colored flat plastic threads into a box pattern.

Lila approached her bed. "Are you going to swim?" she asked.

"I wasn't planning on it."

"Come on, Reena, you're the best swimmer we've got."

"Funny, this morning you were better off without me." Reena focused on her lanyard.

Lila sat down. "Reena—"

"What? I was hurt, and all you cared about was the stupid game."

Lila was fidgeting with her hands. Reena couldn't tell if it was all an act—was Lila trying to say she was sorry, or did she just want to win Color War?

"But you're ok now, right? Your nose, I mean."

"Yeah."

"I know I can't make you swim. But we need you now. Please."

The other day Lila had called her cold and selfish. Maybe this was her chance to prove that she wasn't. Besides, she liked that Lila needed her. And she knew she could be more impressive in the water than she was on the volleyball court. Her nose would heal on its own; maybe swimming could heal her pride.

"Ok." She put her suit on and headed with the others to the lake.

The swimming races were organized by swim class, so Reena swam out to the deep raft with Ellen and the regular crew.

"Ok, teams, we're doing a relay," Ellen said. "Decide amongst yourselves who's swimming what stroke."

The Blue team, which included Reena, Ethan, and Gail, gathered on one side of the raft. Gail wanted to swim breast, and Ethan backstroke. So Reena took free.

"It's not fair," Gail said. "They have two boys and we only have one."

They evaluated the White team, made up of Sam, Jeff, and Michael.

"We're going to kick their asses," Ethan said. "They don't have Reena on their team."

"Me?" Reena said. Just hearing him say her name made her knees weak. But she wasn't sure if he was being sincere, or making a joke. Everything was so different in camp than it had been on the canoe trip. There were so many people around, watching. Everything was an act.

"Time's up," Ellen said. "Backstrokers in the water, breaststrokers on deck. Freestylers bring it home. We're swimming to the outer buoy and back. Swimmers can't get in the water until their teammate has touched the raft. Capeesh?"

"Go White!" Michael said.

"Go Blue!" Gail said.

"Three, two, one . . ." Ellen blew her whistle. Ethan and Sam flew off, a mess of crashing water over their heads. Sam took the lead at first but then he veered off course, and must not have heard his teammates shouting at him. Ethan returned to the raft a half-length ahead, and Gail dove in. Reena watched her head bobbing in and out of the water at an accelerated clip. She was doing well, but Michael was catching up. Michael was the one with real racing experience, and by the time the two girls returned to the raft, Gail had lost their lead.

Reena dove in and swam for her life. She hardly even breathed. Why did it matter to her so much, the outcome of this race? She swam like it was the Olympics, like there would be a medal and a podium at the end. Turning around at the buoy and realizing it was almost over, she turned the engines on even more. As she approached the raft, she could sense Jeff to her right, coming in close. She put her head in and kicked, her arms outstretched. She touched the raft and heard shouts from above. Then she saw Ethan, hands on his knees, shaking his wet head back and forth.

"The White team takes it!" Ellen said.

"Go, White, Go!" Michael chanted, triumphant. Gail hung her head; her cheeks flushed from the swim.

Reena, still in the water, looked up at Ethan. "Damn. I gave you guys the lead!" he shouted. And then he turned away.

She may as well have had a second ball in her face. Reena felt like she could do nothing right.

20
Naomi

Naomi rolled out of bed, sleepy-eyed, and went to services. It was required for all counselors and staff to attend morning *t'filot*, but since swim staff could attend services with any of the divisions, it was easy to skip without anyone noticing. But she'd started feeling a sense of calm and satisfaction during prayers that she'd not had in a long time, and so she went almost every day.

She sang the tunes that she'd been hearing for years with new feeling, sometimes closing her eyes and swaying back and forth like the old men in her parents' synagogue. It was easy, she knew, to get through the monotony by daydreaming as the time passed, hardly present even as she stood and sat, sang and turned pages. But lately she felt she could let loose more than she remembered; she was discovering how to experience the familiar tunes and words in a more active way. Praying in this way reminded her of being with the mystery man in the woods, but also of other experiences—dancing for hours with friends at an outdoor concert on campus that spring, and the moment of clarity last semester when, like clouds floating away to reveal the sun, *To the Lighthouse* had begun to make sense.

After services, Naomi waited until almost everyone had left for breakfast, then she walked over to the cubbies at the side of the Beitan. Hesitantly, she picked up a *tallis* and wrapped it around herself. It felt nothing like a scarf, or any other garment she'd ever worn. It was silky yet steady on her shoulders. She gathered the *tzitzis* up and wrapped them around her fingers. "*V'hayah lakhem l'tzitzit*," she whispered, feeling a connection for the first time to those words from the *Shema* that she'd said countless times: "And they shall be tzitzit for you."

A bench scraped against the floor and Naomi turned around, the *tallis* still on her shoulders.

"Hi, Naomi. Just looking for my sweatshirt. Think I may have left it here."

It was Anne Jacobi, a tall girl with a kind, open face. She was a division head like Mara, and a senior at Barnard. Naomi remembered her from their childhood as a model camper, a girl universally liked. Anne looked at her in the *tallis*.

"Hi." Naomi wasn't sure what else to say. Should she explain what she was doing? She wasn't sure herself.

"Looks good on you," Anne said.

"It feels strange. I've never worn one before. Women don't, at my parents' *shul*," Naomi said.

"I don't buy it that only boys and men can have the full experience of prayer. We can as well."

Naomi didn't answer at first. It had never occurred to her to want to pray like her father and her grandfather. And yet here she was, trying on a *tallis* like a little girl playing dress-up. But wearing it didn't feel like child's play at all.

"I was just seeing what it felt like." She took the *tallis* off and put it back in a cubby.

"Back when women were illiterate and stuck at home, their role was to make babies, and spiritual fulfillment was supposed to come from that. I think we're worth more, don't you?"

"Sure," Naomi said. She'd heard some feminists speak on campus, and Anne's words reminded her of those speeches. She agreed with them on many points: women should get equal pay, and be able to lead full lives independent of men. But she'd never considered the role of women in the synagogue. Maybe that's why she found *shul*, especially her parents' *shul*, boring—women there were spectators, not participants.

"Are you heading to breakfast?" she asked, ready to change the subject.

Anne nodded and they set off together up the dirt path to the dining hall.

"How do you like living in the city?" Anne asked.

"I love New York," Naomi said. "It's like I was waiting all my life to get into the center of things."

"I'm with you there. The city gets into you, under your skin. I really can see myself staying. I mean, after college."

Naomi wondered if she would stay, too. Her parents had moved to Long Island to give their children trees, good public schools, what they thought of as a better life than their own cramped Brooklyn childhoods. But she was beginning to think of herself as a city girl. An image flashed across her mind of herself, ten years in the future, giving a tour at the Met.

"Have you chosen a major?" Anne asked.

"Art history. But I've started thinking I might minor in fine arts. My mother says I should do something useful like Mara—she's doing elementary ed." Naomi smiled. "Between you and me, I'm not even sure if she wants to teach. I think if she gets married she'll probably stay home."

"Maybe. I know she really wants to find Mr. Right. She seems to be enjoying the company of the new music man, what's his name? Jim? They've been working together on the music festival. I haven't seen Mara so happy all summer. Have you noticed?"

"No, I haven't." Naomi lied. She had noticed, and she didn't like hearing about it from Anne. She had convinced herself that Jim must be only looking for friendship, not romance. The idea that he might actually have chosen Mara over her filled her with a cascade of feelings: jealousy, anger, self-loathing. She wasn't sure she could be happy for Mara, if Jim turned out to be hers. She was sure that made her a bad person.

"I could be wrong. You know your sister better than me."

Naomi shrugged. "She hasn't mentioned anything to me."

"So what about you?" Anne said, as they approached the doors to the dining hall. "I've heard there might be a romance for you this summer, too? But it's all very hush hush."

"Who said that?" Naomi said, taking a deep breath.

"Oh, I don't know," Anne said, smirking. "It was nice chatting with you. I better get in there now." She pointed at the dining hall. "Don't worry, I won't say anything."

Anne slipped through the doors and into the mayhem of breakfast. Naomi didn't get a chance to explain, not that she would have known how to, anyway.

21
Reena

Color War began with break out, and ended with the outbreak. In the late afternoon, the whole camp was once again assembled, this time on the baseball field between the girls' and boys' cabins. Excited, overtired kids belted out their team cheers for the last time. Just like when she and her dad watched the Olympics on TV, Reena was surprised how much she wanted her team to win. She thought that maybe if Blue won, Ethan might congratulate her; maybe even hug her. And though it may have been irrational, she felt like it would be her fault if they lost.

There was a delay in the announcement because one of the White team counselors, standing by the microphone, was suddenly sick. Rabbi Warren ushered her aside, and returned to the microphone to make the big announcement. "Let's get this over with. And the winner is . . . BLUE!"

"Yes!" Reena yelled, and turned around, looking for people to celebrate with. Lila danced hand in hand with the other girls wearing blue, and Reena went over to them, but no one opened the circle to let her in. *It's like I'm not here*, Reena thought.

Then she saw Ethan with his friends, blue and white shirts together, walking back to their cabin. Apparently for the guys it was already over. Ethan didn't turn around, or seem to give a thought to her.

Reena looked for Sharon, and found her with her head down, surrounded by her fellow White captains. They had their arms around each other, holding one another up, looking like they might collapse into tears. She walked over.

"I'm sorry your team lost," Reena said, hoping they could move on now.

"You're sorry? What is that, your way of gloating?" Sharon snapped.

"I wasn't gloating."

"Whatever, Reena. I can't talk to you right now."

"Why? It's over, right?"

"Because, I feel really, really sick right now." Sharon leaned over and put her hands on her knees. Then, without warning, she vomited between her feet. Reena put a hand on her back and offered to take her to the infirmary, but Sharon shook her head, and walked off by herself.

Back in the cabin, Lila was still celebrating, dancing and singing to music coming from someone's iPod. She still didn't say a word to Reena. It was true, then. Lila had asked her to swim in order to win Color War, not out of any sense of contrition. Her cousin had *used* her.

Reena was thinking about what to say to Lila, but she never got the chance to confront her, because within the hour Lila was puking, too. The bug, which came on fast, seemed to start with the captains and radiate out into the divisions. After Lila and a few other girls left for the infirmary, the cabin was eerily calm and quiet. Everyone was worn out from the day of running around in the heat.

Reena felt drained; she needed to sleep. She hurriedly threw the day's mess off her bed and onto Sharon's. As she put her pajamas on, she heard whimpering coming from Margaret's bed.

"Are you OK?" Reena asked. Margaret, lying in her bottom bunk, rolled over and pulled the covers over her head. "If you're sick you should go to the infirmary." Reena started to walk away.

"Not sick. Sick and tired," Margaret whimpered.

"What are you talking about?"

"They went through our stuff."

"What? Who?"

"I came into the cabin earlier and Allie and Michael were going through my things. They had my diary, and were looking through my letters. I was going to kill them, and then Susie came in and told them to cut it out. No punishment or anything, of course."

"What do you mean *our* stuff?" Reena asked.

"After Susie left, they got into your things, too. Flipping through your books and stuff. I tried to stare them down and they just went on the attack. I'm sorry, I didn't know what else to do."

Reena looked at Susie, who was putting on make-up in front of a small mirror hanging by her bed at the opposite end of the cabin, probably awaiting lights out so she could go who-knows-where with the other counselors. She thought about going to her, but she knew by then that Susie would never punish Allie and her friends; she wanted to be liked by them too much.

Margaret started crying again. "This whole place makes me burn. I wanna go home. I hate them, all of them."

"I know what you mean," Reena said, as she started inspecting her belongings. At first, she didn't notice anything amiss. If they'd gone through her stuff, it would be difficult for her to tell, as her cubbies were not the neatest. Tangles of unfolded underwear and unmatched socks spilled onto the floor as she poked around. Her books were all there, and so were her brush and canteen.

Michael was sitting with Allie on a top bunk across the room, watching her and choking on their own giggles. They wanted to see her sweat.

Reena reached under the bed and pulled out her stationery box. She knew immediately that someone had been in the box when she saw her father's two postcards from Japan lying on top. She'd put them on the bottom, underneath the stationery, with the pictures that she'd taken from Lila's house and her dad's emergency money. She flipped, panicked, to the bottom of the box.

The money was gone. And so were the photos.

She sat on her bed and bit her pillow. She had no choice but to work this out herself; Sharon wasn't there to fight for her, and even if she had been, Reena didn't know whose side she was even on anymore. Her stomach ached as she walked over to Allie's bed. A hush came over Michael, though her smirk stayed.

"Did you take something of mine?" Reena spoke quietly. She wanted her things back; she didn't want to cause a scene.

"I don't know what she's talking about," said Allie. "Do you?"

Michael shrugged her shoulders and nervously tugged on her thick red hair.

"Yes, you do. Margaret caught you going through my stuff. And now my money and my pictures are missing."

"You must be smokin' something," Allie said, swinging her legs over the edge of the bed.

"Give them back," Reena said.

"Ten second to lights out!" Susie announced, clueless, still standing in front of the mirror.

"She's really nuts, huh?" Michael said, pointing to Reena and looking at Allie.

"Ethan told everyone how easy you are. But he didn't tell us how nutso you are. Don't deny it," Allie said, giggling. "We're all friends here. We can talk about your mental illness. Heard any voices lately? Feeling a little paranoid?"

Reena stared up at them, at a loss. Inside, she was boiling over.

"Five, four, three, two, one!" Susie said. Then she flicked off the light. "G'night! I'll be checking in with *shmira* and expect to hear that you were on your best behavior." Thwack. The cabin door slammed shut and Susie was gone.

Reena imagined grabbing hold of Allie's metal bunk bed and shaking it until the whole thing crashed to the ground. She wanted to scream at the top of her lungs: GIVE ME BACK MY THINGS YOU CREEPS! She wanted to yell so loud that maybe her father would hear her in Japan.

But she didn't. *Street smarts*, she heard her dad say in her head. There's no point in arguing with someone who is both crazy and aggressive, he'd taught her. The best you can do is get away, stay safe, and when necessary notify the authorities. Allie was the teenage equivalent of a hostile drunk, dominating a world in which the authorities could not care less.

Reena turned around and went back to her bed. She was so tired she could almost give up, just to be able to crawl under her covers.

Why had they said that about her? What had Lila told them? Even worse, what had Ethan said? She thought maybe she *was* going crazy. But if that were the case there was one certain cause for her insanity: camp. She'd been fine before she got there. It had been a huge mistake coming to camp—a mistake with only one possible solution. She had to get out of there.

Surely her father would come rescue her if he could, but he was completely unreachable—her cell phone was useless without service, and even if she could sneak into the staff lounge, where she'd heard there was a payphone, she couldn't just call Japan. She knew Mara would refuse to help, and anyway, she didn't want to go home with her to New Jersey. She wanted to go 'home-home', to her apartment, to New York.

She lay in bed until everyone was asleep. Transported by the music on her iPod, her escape had already begun. It took a long while for the cabin to get quiet, and she must have dozed here and there during the wait. When she saw that Susie was back in the cabin, snoring, she got out of bed and grabbed her backpack, shoving in a couple pairs of underwear and socks, and her toothbrush. She took off her pajamas and put on jeans, a t-shirt, and a black hoodie. Now she could really disappear.

She stood in the middle of the cabin floor, her heart beating fast, as girls slept on all sides of her. She didn't want to leave without the photos; they were important to her. What a strange thing for Allie to steal anyway—why would she want pictures of her family? It made her wonder how long the photos had been missing. Lila had only been in the infirmary for a few hours—it was certainly possible that she'd been involved. If Lila knew that Reena had taken the pictures, she might be furious at her for taking them from her house in the first place. Where could they be? She tiptoed over to Allie's bed and leaned over. Her mouth hung open, as she drooled onto her pillow. The area around her bed was a mess, and Reena didn't even know which were her cubbies. As she hovered above her, Allie rolled over. Reena held her body perfectly still.

She couldn't look for the photos right now—it was too risky. She'd have to go without the pictures—and without the money, too.

Slowly, holding her breath, she opened the squeaky cabin door and closed it behind her. Camp was quiet and still. Even *shmira*, the counselors on night-watch duty, had already gone to bed. She walked behind the girls' cabins on the outside of the circle, past the gazebo, and down the lower side of the baseball field. At the start of the dirt path that led out of camp, she thought she saw someone on the other side of the field. She put her head down and walked faster. Minutes later, she was squeezing past the metal gate at the camp boundary.

22

Naomi

Naomi saw the angel again during Kabbalat Shabbat. Dressed in white, he was swaying and dancing in the woods beside the basketball courts. Without thinking, she left her seat on the bleachers and followed him.

He stared at her, his blue eyes sparkling in the evening sun. She felt drawn to him, and curious, but not afraid. She wanted to hear more of his mysterious wisdom. But this time he said nothing. Over the rousing sounds of hundreds of voices welcoming the Sabbath together, he was silent. She thought, perhaps, it was an invitation to get closer, so that she could hear. She approached him and reached out a hand. She wanted to touch him, to put her hand on his face. She thought she might kiss him, that maybe this was what he wanted, after all. "Love will find you," he'd said. And *he* had found her: in Washington Square Park, on Blackberry Hill, and again here. But as she reached out to him, he took a step back. So she went closer, feeling emboldened by the loving way that he looked at her.

With an outstretched arm, he directed her back to the services, as he slowly put one foot behind the other, backing away in a sort of light-footed dance.

She turned around just in time to see Jim arriving. She watched him brush his hair out of his eyes, and noticed the way his striped shirt stuck to his back with sweat. She was transfixed by his corporeality. He looked more relaxed than when she usually saw him, down at the lake. She went to him and stood by his side. He winked, and she exhaled. The angel didn't do things like that. Human things. Funny things. With the music of prayer surrounding them, Naomi felt the heat of Jim's arm beside hers. There was no doubt he was real. She stared into the woods and the dancing man was gone.

Mara stood on the stage with the camper who was leading the prayers. She swayed and sang, her prayer book open in her hands, but her eyes glared at Naomi and Jim.

—

"How's it going, Nay?" Jim walked into the art room carrying his guitar. Naomi looked up at him and smiled, wiping the sweat off her forehead with the back of her arm, trying not to get paint in her hair.

"Okay, I think. I'd cover it up until it was finished, but it's a little big for that." He stood beside her and looked down at the giant piece of brown butcher paper laid across the floor.

"I'm bad at this," he said. "What is it?"

She pushed him affectionately, getting paint on his t-shirt. "It's not done." She stared at the work. She'd sketched out the whole scene, but so far she'd only painted the background. She'd spent a long time on the figure at the right. She felt less confident about drawing people, and she wanted to get it right. "I think you'll recognize it when it's finished."

"Hopefully you'll say the same about the music in the festival. I've been practicing with the kids for days, but I told Mara there's nothing I can do when half of them can't carry a tune."

"And what did Mara say?"

"She said have the band play louder."

"You will work your magic, I have no doubt," Naomi said.

"As will you."

"You think?" Naomi looked at the mural, overwhelmed by all she had left to do. She'd got time off from Jay in order to work on it, but she doubted if she could finish it in time.

"I know." He patted her shoulder. "Have to run."

Naomi smiled as he left, thinking how she'd gotten into this position—painting at camp, rather than lifeguarding. Jim had asked more than once to see her drawings, until finally one day after free swim, she'd let him.

"You can't hide these," he'd said, her sketchbook open on his lap.

"I'm not hiding them. I'm just not showing them."

"But they're really good." He'd flipped through the pages, looking at the pictures of her parents' house and yard, and a portrait of her mother. "What I'm saying is, you've gotta share them. Practicing is only one part of making art. The other part is playing. Giving. Showing."

"I don't know," she'd said, grabbing the sketchbook back.

She kneeled down and dipped a brush in the paint. Jim had asked her to make the mural, for the music festival. She had agreed, for him. He was excited when he talked about art, and she wanted him to be excited about her.

Now she was nervous, fear-of-exposure billowing with each brush stroke. But she was also having a ball. It was amazing how the minutes and hours disappeared when she was working, just like when she was a kid in her father's woodshop. She leaned over and did her best to paint the scene the way she saw it in her mind.

23

Reena

The night was still and warm, with a light-giving half-moon rising in the sky. It had been a month since Reena had been on this stretch of country road that connected camp to the closest highway. She remembered sitting in the back seat of Mara's car; it hadn't seemed long from Route 22 to the camp gate, maybe ten minutes. The road looked completely different on foot and at night. The surrounding fields hummed with cicadas and frogs, and she tripped several times on rocks and in holes.

She kept walking. Now that she'd left, there was only one option—she had to get home. She felt like a character in a book, a child refugee escaping war or abuse or hard labor. Or summer camp. What would her father say?

She put her hand in her jeans pocket and felt the six quarters and four dimes that she'd found in the bottom of her backpack, left over from school lunch money. It was all she had. Not enough to pay for the bus, but she had a plan. Once, when her father couldn't come to pick her up from a friend's apartment uptown, he had told her to take a taxi, and he paid the driver when she got home. Her plan was to call her friend Alisa in the city, who would meet her at Port Authority with the money to pay for the bus. Surely the bus driver would allow this, if the taxi driver had. She would call Alisa as soon as she got service on her cell phone. So far, still no bars.

She walked for over an hour, step by step through the darkness. She wondered when her counselors and cabin-mates would notice she was gone. At wake-up?

Or breakfast? Or maybe not until swimming? What would Ethan say? Would he even care? The day came back to her now, in all its length and drama: Lila showing her true colors, Allie crossing the line. How long would it take for anyone to even realize she wasn't there? Thinking of her dad and their apartment and how desperately she wanted to be back where she knew she belonged, she started to tear up.

Stop crying, she told herself. *You'll never make it home if you act like a baby.* She pulled air into her lungs and stood taller, willing herself to be grown up, at least for tonight.

At last Reena saw the lights of an old-fashioned diner ahead, which meant she'd made it to the highway. She'd noticed the diner on the drive up—a shiny metal box that looked like a toy building in the green rural landscape. She felt a mixture of relief— because she was back in civilization, of sorts—and terror. Would the people in the diner see her immediately for what she was, a teenage runaway? Just act like you know what you're doing, she told herself. She let her backpack fall off her shoulder and held it in one hand as she went in. Sitting on a stool at the counter, she grabbed a menu and hid behind it while having a peek around. There were only two customers: a heavy-set man with a baseball cap drinking coffee in one of the booths, and another man at the opposite end of the counter.

No one seemed to even notice her for several minutes, and she put her head down on her hands. She was so tired. Feeling someone standing in front of her, Reena picked up her head.

"What can I getcha?" said a waitress in a light-blue uniform and white apron. Her name, embroidered in curly letters on her uniform, was Helen.

"Coffee, please."

"Nothin' else?"

Reena shook her head, and the waitress walked away. Her creased face and grey hair pulled back in a bun made her look angry—resentful, maybe, about working the night shift. But when Reena saw her dance across the tiny restaurant, bopping to the music coming from a radio in the kitchen, she thought the waitress must be kind; maybe she would help her.

Helen slid an empty white teacup and saucer in front of her, and poured steaming brown liquid from a glass carafe. Reena added as much milk as would fit in the small cup, and then several heaps of sugar, and stirred. The liquid overflowed onto the saucer, and she got nervous again. The waitress was still standing in front of her. She had imagined drinking coffee would make her look older for sure. Being careful not to wince, she took a sip. Even with the milk and sugar, it still tasted a bit like burnt dirt. She had never understood how her dad could drink so much of the stuff.

"Kinda late for you to be out all by ya'self, no?"

Reena had been preparing for this question, but that didn't make it any easier. "I'm, uh, in college. Just heading back to the city. I've been up here visiting friends, but I need to get back for my summer classes at NYU."

Reena looked Helen in the eye and smiled. It's all about confidence. She wasn't sure if the waitress believed her, though. Her face was impossible to read. I can pass for a college student, Reena told herself. Just watch.

"Good coffee," Reena said, taking a sip. "You wouldn't know where the bus to the city stops around here, would you?"

"Sure do," said Helen. "But tonight ain't your night, hon. The next bus ain't leavin' 'til six tomorrah. And it goes from Paulston, a good hour or maybe two if yus walkin'."

Reena couldn't hide her disappointment; her face practically fell into the coffee. Not until six the next morning! Two hours away! What would she do? She knew about the bottomless cup, but she wasn't sure she could sit there until sunrise. She didn't even think she could finish the cup of coffee in front of her.

"These friends o' yus didn't tell ya when the bus was goin'?"

"I just forgot to ask them," Reena said, wishing Helen would walk away. She needed space to figure out her next move. Finally the waitress disappeared behind a half-door into the kitchen.

Reena sat at the counter, taking occasional sips of coffee, thinking. Should she pay for the coffee and leave as soon as possible, so as not to attract more attention? Maybe she could start the walk to Paulston now, and make it last through the night, staying under the radar. She thought of hitchhiking—her dad once told her that he used to hitchhike way back when, but the world was more dangerous now. Or maybe she should settle in for a few hours, take out her book and iPod and make herself comfortable. Helen seemed like someone who might give her a break; she had a hunch she would leave her alone.

Her stomach was churning, so she grabbed her backpack and ran to the bathroom at the end of the counter. She was relieved that there was toilet paper —it was the kind of grimy bathroom that usually didn't have any—and she covered the seat just in time to sit for the outpouring of her insides. She didn't know if it was stress, illness, or five sips of coffee, but something was wrong with her. As she sat hunched over looking at the filthy linoleum floor under her feet, Reena started to cry again. She was sick, exhausted, and longing for her bed, but her bed was impossibly far away.

Toughen up, she told herself, wiping the tears away with toilet paper. You're a New Yorker. She slung her backpack over her shoulder and washed her hands. Her belly felt better; maybe she'd be ok.

She left the bathroom and was returning to her seat at the counter when she saw two state troopers standing by the only door to the diner, talking to

Helen the waitress. The three of them looked at Reena. Reena left some change on the counter, grabbed her backpack, and slipped out the door as quickly as her sluggish body could move.

—

She carried on walking. The highway was nothing more than a quiet country road, deserted at night. She trudged in the grass by the tree line to keep out of sight of the occasional drivers passing by. Walking down a dark stretch of road with fields of tall grass on both sides, Reena felt alone and exposed. Maybe Allie was right. Maybe she *was* crazy, thinking that she could get home to New York City by her feet alone. Her stomach rumbled again, and she thought, desperately, that things actually could get worse.

That was when she heard the footsteps behind her. The sound of feet shuffling over gravel was unmistakable—nothing like the background noise of insects. Someone was on the road with her, and from the sound of it, he or she was catching up. Had someone followed her out of the diner? A townie out for a walk in the middle of the night? Or—she began to panic—could it be an escapee, a resident of the nearby insane asylum? She was considering jumping off the road and into the tall grass, when the footsteps came up right beside her. She spun around, afraid to have her back turned away any longer, and let out a scream.

"Welcome," said the man with the straggly beard, feet bare as always.

"Holy shit! You scared the hell out of me." It was the first time she'd shouted all day. "You can't just sneak up on people like that! For God's sake!" She surprised herself with her fighting spirit. Why couldn't she be so self-assured with Allie and Michael?

"She who invokes the name of the Lord shall do so in righteousness."

"What? I don't understand you, I don't know why you're following me around, and I don't have a clue what you're doing in that photograph with my mother. Who are you?"

There. She'd asked. She'd promised herself if she saw him again she would, and now she had. He would have to explain, or leave her alone. She stood facing him, her hands clutching the straps of her backpack by her shoulders.

"I am God's emissary. I have come to offer a blessing."

"You chased me here in the middle of the night to give me a blessing? I don't want one."

"This path shall lead you astray." He pointed to the road before her, in the direction that she had been heading. "You ask of your mother? Follow in her footsteps."

"I can't follow her, goddammit! She's dead!" Reena stamped her foot.

When she was little, sometimes her father would imitate her temper tantrums, to show her what she looked like when she was carrying on. Of course, it made her embarrassed and angry. But it also worked —as soon as she saw him thrashing about and pouting, she knew she'd gone too far. As the man— who had never done her any wrong—stood there calmly, she saw herself as a grouchy three-year-old.

"*Y'varech'cha Adonai v'yish-m'recha,*" he sang. "May the Lord bless you and keep you." He held his hands at his side, and swayed. Like the first time she'd met him, Reena was carried away by the clarity of his voice and the sweetness of the melody.

"*Ya-ir Adonai panav eilecha vichuneka.*" He put his hands over her shoulders, and she felt her temperature rise. "May the Lord cause His spirit to shine upon you and be gracious unto you."

Then, circling around her, he sang: "*Yisa Adonai panav eilecha v'yaseim l'cha shalom.* May God turn His spirit unto you and grant you peace."

He began to sing his comforting, lilting, circular tune, and she realized that during the time he'd been with her, she'd no longer felt alone, or scared. He spun her in a circle, giving her a clear view in both directions each time she turned around—the road back to the diner, and to camp, where she had come from, and the road ahead, to Paulston and New York, where she had been heading.

"You shall discover God's truth. Remember, to lose one's way is to find another." Singing again, he walked off the road and into the field, disappearing into the thick grass and trees.

Reena wasn't sure if she felt abandoned or relieved.

Her head was spinning. The man—if he was a man—had known her mother. If only she still had the picture, to prove it to herself—to make things clear. He was trying to tell her something. What did it mean: follow her mother's footsteps? Reena spun around and around, humming the man's tune, her circular steps in time with the rhythm of the melody that vibrated through her veins.

Then she saw the lights of a police car, driving very slowly in her direction. She had time to duck into the tall grass and hide. But instead, she waved her arms above her head, standing in the middle of the road. Her mother had been in camp; had known this man, whoever, whatever he was, in camp. Maybe he was telling her she needed to go back.

24

Naomi

The next afternoon, the staff lounge was buzzing with news of the evening plan. There would be a concert on a nearby ski hill, and though no one was sure who the headliner was—the rumor was Dylan would be there—the line-up was sure to be good. Naomi wanted to go. The concert sounded like the perfect change of routine, after days and weeks of lifeguarding. And she wanted Jim to take her.

She glanced across the messy rec room, with its beat-up sofas and snack table set with bug juice and sugar cookies, to where Jim was playing ping-pong with Greg. She was about to go over to them when Mara put a hand on her back.

"Naomi, can I talk to you a minute?" she said.

"Sure."

Mara grabbed her hand and pulled her out to the porch. "I know you've been working on the mural for the music festival."

"Yeah, Jim asked me to—"

"I know. This is about him."

"What about him?"

"Well, we've been spending a lot of time together getting the campers ready, and ever since I met him, I don't know, I just felt like he's different. You know? He doesn't care what people think of him, and he's just nothing like all those Brandeis boys waiting in line to become their dads. And he's so cute. I just can't stop thinking about him."

"Oh." Naomi felt a knot tighten in her stomach. "So?"

"So, are you okay with that?"

"With what?"

"Just, I don't know. You've not exactly been forthcoming with your love life this summer. If you're even having one. So I didn't know what you'd think. You know, because you've been hanging out with him, too."

Naomi wasn't sure what Mara wanted her to say. Did she want her permission to date Jim? It wasn't really hers to give.

"Are you together? You and Jim? Because he's not really what I pictured as your type."

"What's that supposed to mean?"

"Forget it."

"Don't act all superior, Naomi. You've been doing that all summer. It's not *my* fault that you had a fight with mom and dad and things didn't work out the way you wanted. Everything isn't always my fault."

"I never said it was."

Mara twirled a long curl around her finger. "Jim's taking me to the concert at Pike's Peak tonight," she said.

"What?" Naomi looked through the window at Jim just as he caught the ping-pong ball. "I'm a little surprised you're interested."

"Well stop being so surprised. Everyone's talking about the concert. The guys in the band were talking about it this afternoon. They're all going, and Jim offered to take me, too. He's got a car, you know."

"I meant interested in Jim."

"Well, glad we had this chat, then. Wish I had more time, but I have to run a staff meeting in five. See you later, Sis." Mara leaned in and kissed Naomi on the cheek.

Naomi sat down on the porch. She couldn't believe Mara, trying to bulldoze over her and yet still planting kisses on her like nothing at all had just happened.

Naomi knew there was energy between her and Jim. She could feel it. But she had to admit it was odd that they'd been in camp for weeks, and he hadn't done anything to indicate for sure that he was interested in her.

Still, if the guys in the band were going too, then it wasn't exactly like Mara had a 'date' with Jim. She stood up and went back inside the staff lounge.

"Hey, Jim," Naomi said. "Do you have room for extras in that big boat of yours tonight?"

"For you, Nay? 'Course I do," Jim said. "We can squeeze a few more in the way back, too."

"Perfect," Naomi said.

—

That evening, after their charges were in bed and their one free night of the week had begun, Naomi and Jennifer skipped excitedly down to the parking lot wearing flower crowns that they had made that afternoon. In a bright red t-shirt and her favorite jeans, Naomi was doing her best not to care about Mara's territorial behavior. She was going to have fun anyway.

"Wait, is everyone leaving already?" she heard a voice call from across the path. She couldn't see the speaker's face because the area was poorly lit, but she knew who it was.

"We're heading down to the parking lot," Jennifer answered.

Mara approached them, still wearing her Shabbat skirt.

"Are you coming?" Jennifer continued.

Naomi dipped her head back, pretending to look up at the sky. She didn't want to answer questions about how she was getting there.

"Yes, I'm coming," Mara said. "Tell Jim to wait for me! I just need to change and grab my camera. I haven't had time to take pictures all summer. I'll be right back."

She ran off, and they continued on to the parking lot.

Jim was sitting on the hood of his beat-up blue Mazda, playing guitar. Naomi approached him and he raised his eyes to her.

"Hey, Nay." He laughed. "Is that a song? If not it should be. Hey, hey, hey, Nay. Hey, hey, hey, Nay." He played around, finding some chords to go along with his new composition.

"Wow, you should write for the radio," Naomi said, smiling.

"Excellent career advice. So, are we going? Where's Mara?"

"She's not ready, yet."

"That's cool. We can wait." He jumped off the car and put the guitar in the back seat. Then he went back to the hood and took a package of rolling papers out of his jeans pocket.

He patted the spot next to him and Naomi climbed up and watched him roll a joint and light up, as if he were in his own backyard. What would Mara say to that?

He passed it to her and she took a drag and held it out to Greg, who passed it on to Jennifer who was lying in the grass near the car. Naomi hoped no one noticed that she'd only done this a few times before. They sat like that for a while, passing the joint until it was a tiny stub. Then Jim rolled another.

Jennifer started singing, "I'm leaving on a jet plane. . ." and they all joined in. Naomi was so happy, and they'd not even left yet. She could feel the heat of Jim's arm beside hers, and wanted to touch it, to feel both its softness and strength. She was afraid that, if they didn't go, somehow the night might end too soon. They needed to get out of camp, to make sure that they had an adventure.

"Come on, let's go," she said.

"You sure? What about Mara?" Jim asked, raising an eyebrow.

"Yes, I'm sure. She probably got tied up in a disciplinary action or planning tomorrow's staff meeting." Everyone laughed, and Naomi felt a pang of remorse. She felt like she was on autopilot, doing things she didn't mean to do and saying things she didn't mean to say, but it was too late. She couldn't go back.

"If you say so," Jim said. And they all piled into the car and sped away down the dirt road, through the gates, and into the outside world.

25

Reena

Sitting in the back seat of the police car was surreal. At least they didn't handcuff her. One of the troopers, round-faced and mean-looking, got into the front behind the steering wheel and turned the engine on, though the car stayed parked in the lot beside Eve's Diner.

"What's your name?" asked the other one, a balding guy with a long mustache. He sat next to Reena in the back seat, holding a notebook.

"Reena Halpern."

"Age?"

"Fourteen."

"Where are you runnin' from, honey?"

"I was going home. I live in Manhattan."

"Oh, sure you do, all the runaways wanna live in the big city," said the driver, without turning around.

"Stay out of it, Douglass," said the mustached man, and then: "So watcha doin' up in Dutchess County?"

"My dad made me come to this camp, but, but . . ." But, what? She couldn't exactly tell them that she was a refugee from the nastiness of a bunch of mean girls.

"Name of the camp?" he asked her, shaking his head. Then, to Douglass: "We get a couple of these every summer, with all the camps up 'round the lakes. Makes you wonder why these city kids just don't stay put, 'stead of comin' up here in the first place."

"Camp Tova." The pains in her stomach were returning; feeling drained, she leaned her head against the seat.

"Will be a helluva wake up call for the folks that run that place—their kids gettin' out in the middle of the night." He jumped out of the backseat and got in the front. "C'mon, Douglass, movin' on out."

From the backseat of the police car, the dirt road to camp looked different yet again. The officers talked to each other and on their walkie-talkies. Reena looked out at the horizon, trying not to be sick. The moon had set behind the trees by this time, and the night was very black, with lots of stars. The car came to a halt outside the camp gate. Someone must have called ahead because there were a handful of camp administrators waiting for them, including Rabbi Warren, the camp director, and Sharon's mother Anne.

Anne brought Reena to her office, a small windowless room with fluorescent lighting and peeling paint, and told her to sit and stay; she'd be right back. Reena assumed that she and Rabbi Warren were still talking to the policemen, maybe filling out paperwork. She wondered what would happen to her, but also if the camp would get in trouble. She was surprised that she'd been left alone at all, after what she'd done.

She sat in the hard plastic chair across from Anne's desk, clutching tightly to the seat with both hands to keep herself upright. After a minute or two, she put her head down on Anne's desk, resting her left cheek beside a mugful of pens and pencils. She kept her eyes open, and in this position discovered a photograph, framed and hung crooked on the bare white wall. It was a wide shot of camp from above—it must have been taken from a plane or a helicopter—and she could easily pick out the dining hall, the steps to the lake, and the baseball diamond. A caption read: "Camp Tova, rural retreat for Jewish children of the New York Metropolitan Area, c 1988." It felt like a glimpse backward in time, and yet the buildings and the landscape looked exactly the same: there was the dining hall, the lake, and the circles of girls' and boys' cabins. Her mother could have been inside one of the cabins at the time the photo was taken. She would probably have heard the engines of the low-flying small plane; maybe she even looked out the window and pointed it out to a friend.

Reena heard footsteps and sat up straight. The sudden movement nauseated her.

"Reena Halpern. I could ask you what is going on, but I think I know." Anne used a stern, business-like voice. She sat down in the chair behind the desk, facing her.

"You do?"

Anne nodded. "I've just had a talk with Rabbi Warren, who would like to call your aunt right now and have her pick you up."

"My aunt?" A chill went down Reena's back.

"Yes, your father listed Mara Stein as your emergency contact, and made it clear he would be unreachable throughout the summer." She looked at a file on her desk as she spoke.

Reena couldn't believe how her errors in judgment were piling up. Now she might end up with the worst of outcomes: being sent to Mara. Mara wouldn't want her around, spoiling her child-free summer. She pictured herself as Cinderella, forced to sleep in the attic and scrub the house. But then maybe Mara would call her father and demand that he come home?

For the first time, Reena realized that would make her father furious with her, too, ruining his big tour. She felt sweaty, and saliva pooled at the back at her mouth. She leaned over and vomited on the dusty floor. The substance that came up was dark and acidic, smelling faintly of diner coffee.

"Oh my, Reena! You're sick!" Anne said, getting up. She brought Reena a cup of water and a paper towel, and put an arm around her shoulders. With her other hand, Anne felt her forehead.

"Thank you," Reena whispered, taking a sip of water. The liquid burned the back of her throat. "Don't call Mara. Please. I'm really sorry."

"Reena, what are we supposed to do with you? We

can't just have campers walking out the gate. If you have a problem, talk to your counselor, talk to me. What you did is not acceptable."

"I'm sorry." Reena didn't know if it would help to say it again, but she wanted Anne to believe her—anything to avoid Mara and her certain anger and disappointment. She really was sorry, not for running away, exactly, but for having done it so badly. She was sorry for having woken Anne in the middle of the night, and for having thrown up on her floor. She was sorry Anne had been assigned to solve this impossible problem—her.

Anne picked up the phone on her desk. *She's doing it*, Reena thought; *she's calling Mara.* She covered her mouth with the paper towel, hyperventilating to hold back the tears. Everything she'd been trying so hard to keep together was falling apart.

"Hi. Anne Jacobi-Baum. I need maintenance in my office please. Yes, and let the infirmary know there will be a new admission this evening." She hung up and said, "I'm taking you to the infirmary and expect you to stay put. I'll come talk to you in the morning."

"Thank you," Reena said, through tears. She didn't know if Anne would also call Mara, or if it would be her last night in camp, but she knew that for the moment she wasn't being punished, and that she would soon be able to get into bed. It was hard to believe after the day she'd had, but she felt relieved to be allowed to sleep in camp that night.

26

Naomi

In the final approach to Pike's Peak, the traffic on the narrow two-lane country road slowed to a crawl.

"Looks like we walk from here," Jim said, pulling over and throwing the car into park. For some reason that made Jennifer laugh, and soon they were all breathlessly giggling.

They piled out and began walking through the thick soup of people and cars; the road had become a parking lot, people hanging out of open car windows, singing and shouting. The distant vibration lured the crowd, which moved as one towards the source of the noise as though under a spell.

It was difficult to move amongst so many people, and Naomi grabbed hold of Jim's hand in front of her, and Jennifer's behind. She felt tightness in her chest, as if there wasn't enough air to breathe, and a buzzing around her scalp.

At the front of the line, Greg shouted, "Follow me!"

"Where are we going?" Jennifer asked.

"Trust me," Greg said.

They followed him up a grassy embankment and onto a dark wooded path where it was much quieter. Naomi took deep breaths, and focused intently on keeping herself upright on the uneven ground. How had she never realized how difficult walking could be? Jennifer started singing again. Her voice was smooth and high like a bell, and Naomi focused on its clear sound to lead her.

The rocky path widened to become a steep, unpaved lane cut through the trees. The group walked side-by-side in the moonlight. The music got louder and louder as they climbed the hill, until they emerged from the trees and had a view of a wide slope covered in people, with a lit-up stage at the bottom. A smile crept across Naomi's face. They were in!

Greg turned to face them, pleased with himself. "I used to ski here. Had a feeling Bear Run would be easier than fighting the crowds."

"Well, you were right, my man," said Jim. "C'mon."

They let go of each other and skipped down the hill. Naomi felt a buzzing behind her ears as they came to the back edge of the audience and stopped, watching and listening. It wasn't Dylan on the stage, but a girl singer with short blonde hair, and two guys with guitars.

Naomi closed her eyes and shut out the world. She felt kinship with the instant community around her. It didn't matter if you were a lifeguard or a grad student, a janitor or a principal, married or still living with your parents; they were all one and the same standing on that hill in the humid night.

When she opened her eyes, Naomi could only focus on one thing: Jim. She could hardly look away. He moved to the music in a relaxed way, listening more than dancing. And while he was absorbed in the music, Naomi found herself absorbed in him. Trying to hear what he was hearing, she focused on the sounds of the guitars and the harmonizing voices; she let the melodies envelop her. She was physically attuned to the distance between them, and when she danced, she moved closer and closer, so that her arms occasionally brushed his chest. His body heat mixed with the warmth of the night and with her own rising fever.

"Let's go closer! I want to get up front." Jennifer grabbed Naomi's hand and tugged.

Naomi let Jennifer lead her towards the stage, into the thick of the crowd. The bodies were dense, and it was surprisingly intimate, touching so many strangers to make their way through. Naomi felt Jennifer's slender fingers slip away from hers. Her head was foggy from the weed, and there were so many people. She spun around, admiring the beautiful faces all around her. But then she realized that the people around her, though familiar-looking, were not her friends; any one of them could have been Jim or Greg or Jennifer, but none of them were.

She turned around and pushed through the throngs, trying to retrace her steps. Where was everyone? Where was Jim? She ran back up the hillside to get a better vantage point. Her heart beat so loudly she thought it might drown out the band.

Feeling exhausted, she let her legs collapse under her and sat in the grass. "Where are you?" she cried, continuing to scan the masses below.

"God's presence can be felt in all corners."

Naomi recognized the voice. She didn't, at this moment, feel at all surprised. Of course he was here. She looked at him, with his beard and bare feet, and thought how well he blended in at this bohemian gathering.

"I'm lost," she said.

"Do not despair. God will show you the way."

"I'm not looking for God," she said, sounding more bitter than she intended.

"Follow your heart—"

"I'm trying. I am. But I don't know where it's leading me." She shook her head and lay down on the ground, gazing at the sky as if it might hold an answer.

He leaned over her, his gentle face obscuring her view of the moon, and started singing. Though unrelated to the music streaming uphill from the stage, his song wove seamlessly with those sounds. Naomi closed her eyes and sang with him.

She felt herself come alive again. Though she felt woozy, she kept singing, looking at the man beside her, wondering what to make of him. *Are you an angel?* she thought. She rose to her feet and they began to dance.

You know why I'm here, he told her without speaking. *You found* me. *You are a seeker of God's truth.*

Is this about the tallis? About prayer? What about love?

Follow your heart.

Then he sang louder, and he danced faster, putting his arm around Naomi to draw her in. But though they touched, she could hardly feel him; unlike Jim, he gave off no heat.

Naomi heard someone shout her name, and looked up as a flash of light blinded her.

Then Mara appeared from behind a Polaroid camera.

"How did you get here?" Naomi asked. She felt light-headed and sick to her stomach.

"Damn you, Naomi. You left me! Luckily some counselors from my division were heading out and they squeezed me in." Mara grabbed the print from the camera and waved it back and forth.

"I'm sorry," Naomi said. "We waited a while and you didn't come. I thought you changed your mind."

"Well I made it, no thanks to you. But where is everyone? What are you doing up here by yourself?"

She turned around. She hadn't even felt him slip away, but he was gone.

"Let's go," Mara said. "We need to find the others before we get left here."

Mara linked her arm into her sister's and started pulling her. Naomi resisted. She wasn't ready to leave. She was still thinking of the angel. Where had he gone?

"I don't understand," Mara said. "Do you realize Jim is scouring the hillside looking for you? Why are you just standing here? What is going on?"

"Jim's looking for me?" Naomi felt dizzy.

"I should have known. I'm such a fool."

"What happened, Mara?" Naomi stopped and looked at Mara. The crowd roared.

"Like I said, I'm a fool. Jim is always so sweet to me; I . . . I misunderstood. When I found him tonight, when I saw the way he was desperate to find you . . ." Mara started crying.

Naomi grabbed Mara's shoulders and pulled her close.

"He's in love with you!" Mara shouted, spraying saliva and tears and pulling away. "Of course he is. You're charming and lovely. You can be whoever you like: the sexy lifeguard, the studious art-lover, the downtown hipster. You have some guy stashed away in your secret place in the woods, and still Jim loves you. You don't know what it's like when there are responsibilities, expectations. We can't all be free like you."

Naomi felt like her sister was breathing fire in her face. But she couldn't fix it, not now. *He's in love with you.*

"Where is he?"

"I don't know," Mara said, sniffing. "Please, Naomi, don't run off again."

"I have to find Jim. I know I'll find him this time." *I'll follow my heart*, she thought. "Wait for me at the top of the hill, where you found me before. I'll come back. Promise."

Naomi started off into the crowd, but then felt a pang of remorse. Had she just blithely stabbed her sister in the heart? She turned around. "I'm sorry," she called, but Mara didn't hear.

Weaving through the hordes, Naomi hummed the angel's tune like a mantra. Maybe a minute, maybe an hour later, she felt a set of strong fingers wrap around her wrist.

"Where have you been?" Jim said. He pulled her close to him, and his warmth radiated through her. "Naomi." Her name sounded musical when he said it, the way he held the sticky vowels.

"I've been looking for you," she said. "And here you are." She smiled, and he kissed her upturned lips.

Thank you, God, she thought. *And your messenger.*

27

Reena

Reena's admission to the infirmary was quick—none of the usual waiting in line that takes place during "sick call", when campers line up for a turn to tell the nurses their medical woes. A heart-faced nurse named Carol took her temperature and handed her a cup with two white pills to swallow. Then she led her through the infirmary, past locked glass-fronted cabinets full of medicine, by a small kitchen that smelled of coffee, and to a room with several bunk beds, marked "Girls" on the outside like a restroom. Whispering, she said, "only one bed left—the top one in the corner."

Reena didn't have pajamas or a toothbrush, but she didn't care. She climbed into bed and pulled the plain white sheets over her head, and fell into a dreamless sleep.

She awoke the next morning and heard sounds that she couldn't place—the hum of an air conditioner, the squeak of footsteps, the voices of unfamiliar women. She opened her eyes and remembered the police car, Anne's office, and the nurse. The room was bright, and she assumed she must have slept half the day away, but when she opened her eyes she saw that most of the other girls were sleeping; it must still be morning.

There was Lila, in the bed beside her own, her curls covering her face. Reena remembered that Sharon was in the infirmary, too, and rolled onto her stomach to peek over the edge of her bed to the one below. Sure enough, there was Sharon, lying on her back, eyes open.

"Reena?" she whispered, sitting up. "When did you get here?"

"Last night." Reena's voice was hoarse, and her head hurt.

"I'm surprised I didn't notice you coming in. I was back and forth to the bathroom all night."

"It was late," Reena said, realizing that she needed the toilet now, and quick. She swung her legs over the edge of the bed and dropped herself to the floor. When she got back from the bathroom, Sharon patted the space next to her on the bed, so she sat.

"I'm so sorry, Reena. I know I was really busy the last few days, and I didn't mean to ignore you like that. I found out about getting captain a couple days ago, and there were all these top-secret meetings, and I just got wrapped up, I guess. I was so, so bummed when I found out you weren't on my team."

Reena sat there, listening to her, but she wasn't sure what to say. It felt good to sit next to her.

"And, oh, that volleyball game!" Sharon continued. "Are you okay? Oh, man, I'm such a bitch. Here I am, asking you how you are *now*, an entire day too late. I'm really sorry, Reena."

Though she was still wearing her dirty sweatshirt and jeans from the night before, Reena felt washed in comfort. She had a friend, a good friend. How could she have left without even saying goodbye to her?

"Sharon, I think this may be my last day here." Reena told her all that had happened, from the fight with Allie and Michael through to her arrival at the infirmary in the middle of the night. "What do you think your mom will do?"

Sharon took Reena's hand. "What do you want her to do?"

"Last night, I wanted out of here more than anything. But then, out there, I felt lost, like I was making a mistake." Her eyes hidden in her wild hair, Reena looked down at her lap.

"You need to stay here with me," Sharon said.

"There's lots of stuff left this summer, and you don't want to miss the play, and the music festival, and the banquet. You have to stay, Reena. I need you."

I need you too, Reena thought. She felt she was meant to stay in camp, now. If it wasn't already too late. "I think your mother may have already called my Aunt Mara by now. She'll probably show up here any minute and tell me to go pack my bags."

"What's that about my mom?" asked Lila, who, still lying down, had turned her head to face them. How much had she heard? The air-conditioner—one of the only ones in camp—whizzed above their heads.

Fast on her feet, Sharon said, "We heard they might be calling the parents of the sick kids, and Reena was just saying they would call your mom for her."

"That's stupid," Lila said. "Why would they call our parents just because we're sick? No one's dying or anything."

"Yeah, totally," said Sharon, squeezing Reena's hand.

They went out to the kitchen, where sick campers were eating breakfast with the nurses, and brought sweetened tea in Styrofoam cups back to their beds. None of the nursing staff seemed to know about Reena's escape attempt, and it felt strange to her to be treated no differently than any of the other campers, after all that. She kept thinking they'd put her in shackles, or make her wear a scarlet letter. Also, there was no sign of Anne, who had promised to continue their conversation in the morning.

At nine, and then again at noon, the nurses came to each bed and took everyone's temperature, handing out Tylenol to anyone with a fever above 99. You could return to your cabin once you had three normal temps in a row, and hadn't vomited in 24 hours; after each temperature check, one or two campers would grab their things and leave. Since Lila and Sharon and Reena had all been sick the night before, they weren't going anywhere that day. They were the only girls from their cabin, and as Reena sat on the bed and whispered to Sharon, she was conscious of leaving Lila out. She wondered how that felt to her cousin, and if she cared.

—

After lunch, they were lying on their beds reading old magazines when Anne walked through the glass-paneled door into the girls' sick room. She was wearing a faded yellow camp t-shirt and khaki shorts.

"Eema!" Sharon sat up and held her arms out to her mother.

Anne gave her a kiss and hug, and said, "How are you, Sweetie?"

"Better, I think," Sharon replied. From the top bed Reena couldn't see what happened next, but she thought Sharon was whispering to her mother, because she didn't hear them say anything for a few minutes. Finally, Anne stood up.

"Reena, can I talk to you for a moment, please? I actually came here to see you, too."

Reena followed Anne into one of the exam rooms. It had a doctor's table covered with paper, a small desk, and a poster tacked to the wall that said: "Be a Germ Buster. Wash Your Hands."

Leaning against the exam table, Anne gestured for Reena to sit in the chair. "Why did you leave camp last night?" she asked.

Reena rubbed her sweaty palms together, and shrugged her shoulders. "I don't know." She couldn't imagine telling Anne that she had felt so completely alone that it seemed better to leave. She was afraid Anne would think less of her—that she was a head case, and a bad friend for Sharon. But perhaps that damage was already done.

"Do you want to stay?" Anne crossed her arms. She seemed frustrated, but also concerned.

"Yes."

"But last night you apparently did not?"

Reena shrugged.

"Look, Reena. I'm going to level with you. I don't think you're a bad kid. I know you're not. And I know it's not been easy being the new girl in the group. But if I'm going to argue that you should be allowed to stay, I need to know that you're not going to pull another stunt like this. I need to know that you're going to follow the rules."

Reena nodded. This was her moment to plead, she realized. Now's when she should say how glad she is to be at camp, and that she made a terrible mistake, and that all she wanted was to finish out the summer. But could she say these things honestly? She still would have preferred to be at home in New York. Except, as the barefoot man had reminded her, her mother was here in camp—present in the buildings and landscape that remained from her day—if only she knew how to find her.

"Did my mother like camp?" she asked. She'd been trying for some time to picture her mother in these surroundings. Had she been popular? Had she been Color War captain? Was she good at volleyball? So many questions Reena had never thought to ask before.

Her father always told the same stories about her mother—how she had impressed all their friends with her homemade Mexican feasts; how when she decided to make part of their apartment into her studio, she gave away all but one pair of shoes to make room for art supplies, which filled their closet; how once, on the way home from the market, she tripped and dropped two dozen eggs on the sidewalk, and she sat down and cried until he walked by, and then they both started laughing. These stories never changed, and they were repeated to Reena, year after year—the Mexican feast story whenever they had burritos; the shoe story whenever Reena asked for new ones; the egg story whenever she became overly upset about something. It was like the memories of her mother had been turned into fables. She wasn't a real person. She was a myth. Anne was the first person she'd ever met who had known her mother in a totally different way.

If her question surprised Anne, she didn't show it. "Naomi seemed very happy to me, Reena. She was down by the lake most days, which means I didn't spend all that much time with her. But I remember the summer that she met your father."

"You do?"

"Oh, yeah. A *lot* happened that summer. You'd be surprised, but things that happen in camp stick with you for a long time. I like to say that's because in camp, time is compressed—a year's worth of relationships happen in eight weeks. It's true every summer."

"I can't imagine her. I want to know her, and I can't."

"No, I don't suppose you can." Anne knelt down and took Reena's hand. "You can't remember this, and perhaps no one has ever told you. When your mother passed away, the whole camp community mourned her. Her funeral was full of her friends from camp, and those people never got a chance to be a part of your life, because she was the connection between you and them. Your being here this summer is like a return of sorts—a return of your family to the place where you began."

"I have never felt like this place was mine." Though as soon as Reena said it she knew it wasn't true. She had felt it on the lake, and in the clearing on the hill. Even today, in the infirmary, she'd felt it a little.

On Visiting Day, parents came to camp to see their children; maybe she had come to camp to see her parents. Maybe that's what the barefoot man had meant when he said, "Follow in her footsteps."

"I want you to stay here, Reena," Anne said. "I truly believe camp is a good place for kids, or I wouldn't work here. And I want you to see that, too. I want camp to be a special home for you, just as it is for my family, and as it once was for yours. So can we make a deal?"

Reena looked down at Anne, still crouching beside her. She wasn't sure she deserved this amount of kindness. "Yes."

"Good. You promise me that I won't get any more emergency calls pertaining to your whereabouts, and I'll keep Mara out of this."

"You haven't called her?" Reena let out a deep breath.

"So do we have a deal?"

"Yes."

Anne patted Reena's knee, and sent her back to the sick room, where she jumped on Sharon's bed, feeling better already.

Reena was so grateful to Anne for trusting her, and for keeping the whole running away episode from Mara, that she took seriously her promise to be good.

"You need to help keep me out of trouble," she whispered to Sharon in the dining hall, over a breakfast of rock-hard pieces of French toast doused in fake maple syrup. "Be my guardian angel."

"Ok," Sharon laughed, "do I get wings and a halo?"

"If you want."

"Not very Jewish."

"Jews don't believe in angels?"

"There are angels in the Torah. They're called *malachim*; messengers, really. They send messages from God. Angels tell Sarah that she's going to have a son, and save Lot from dying."

Reena thought about the barefoot man, who sang and danced and said all those things about blessings and God. On the road, he'd said he was God's emissary. She'd had that word on a vocab test last year. It meant agent, representative, or messenger.

"What do those angels, in the Torah, look like?"

"I think they looked like regular people. I mean, like everyone else in biblical times. Probably wore togas or something."

"No wings."

"Nope."

"Why angels? Can't God just talk to people himself?"

"How? With a burning bush? Unless you're Moses, you'd just run. I think God sends angels because they look like people. Less scary."

"But would everyone know who the angels were?"

"No, only the person receiving the message, I think. No one else would probably even notice them."

Reena wondered if anyone else could see her angel.

Sharon leaned over to Reena and whispered, "We need to see if we can find the stuff they stole from you."

"Yes," Reena whispered back. It was something she'd been thinking about ever since they'd been released from the infirmary. The more time went by, the more Reena wished she'd told Susie about the burglary when it happened. It would seem silly to mention it now, and besides, Allie and Michael would just deny it. It wasn't like the money had her name on it. She'd stayed quiet and angry, imagining how she would indignantly tell her father what happened. (Though she could imagine, too, what he would do: pat her on the back and say, "So now you know. People aren't honest. Keep your money in more than one place.")

Sharon whispered back. "You've heard Allie and Lila scheming, right? Well I think they're gonna do it, tonight. They're going on a raid."

Reena had heard all about the raid. Allie had even asked her, jokingly, if she wanted to go. "C'mon, Reena! Live a little!" But Reena had already experienced sneaking around camp in the dark. She would not put herself at risk again of a phone call to Mara. She would not sneak out in the middle of the night to visit a boys' cabin. There weren't any boys who she wanted to see, anyway; or rather, none who wanted to see her in return.

At least Allie was speaking to Reena, even if it was only ever to tease; ever since they'd all been let out from the infirmary, Lila hadn't said a word to her. Reena could feel the heat of her cousin's anger every time she walked by. She didn't know if it was because Lila had heard about the fight she'd had with her friends. She wondered if it could have anything to do with those missing pictures. Now that Allie and Dan were going out, maybe she was feeling left out. She watched Lila take a sip of juice at the far end of the long dining table. Michael was whispering in her ear.

"Yeah, they haven't been very discreet about the raid, have they?" Reena replied, dipping a bite of cold toast in syrup, and washing it down with milk.

"We won't have a lot of time because my guess is they're gonna get caught—and quick—but when they're out, we'll have a look and see what we can find, OK?"

"OK." Reena pushed her tray away and rested her chin in her hands. She looked at the artwork that hung above the windows. Colorful murals ran the length of the dining hall, giving the room a festive feeling. But she'd never looked closely at them before. One showed a group of children dancing in a circle; one showed a farm; another was clearly a depiction of the lake at camp, complete with floating rafts.

"Who did those?" Reena asked Sharon, pointing.

"I'm not sure. They've always been there. They must have been made a long time ago."

—

That night there was a lot of whispering, and dashing around the cabin, and the ringleaders even put black tights on their heads. Sharon and Reena watched it all with amusement. They waited until the *shmira* counselors were out of sight, and then more than half the girls in the cabin dashed out into the night.

"Quick!" Sharon said.

Reena nervously ran her hands through piles of clothes in Allie's cubbies while Sharon looked through Michael's. It was dark and hard to see, but she knew what she was looking for. "Nothing here. You?"

Sharon shook her head. Reena hesitated in front of Lila's cubbies, but then continued the search. She found Lila's wallet, stashed under her pile of pink underwear. She opened it, and found a few twenties. But there was no way to tell if they were the same ones that had been in her stationery box. Would Lila really steal from her? She didn't know, and without the photos, she had no evidence.

There was a light knock on the wall right beside where Reena was standing. She jumped. "Did you hear that?!"

"No, what?" Sharon said. "They can't be back yet."

Now, through the window, they both heard it. "Reena!"

Sharon looked out. "Reena, um, Ethan Marcus is on the porch."

Reena put Lila's wallet away and pushed the cabin door open. His face was right beside the door.

"Come out," he whispered.

Reena opened the door and slipped outside. She was already nervous from the rush of going through other people's belongings. Now Ethan pulled her by the hand into the shadows, on the grass beside the porch steps, and she thought her heart might leap from her chest.

"I thought you'd be on the raid with the others," he said.

"Me?"

"Yes. Why didn't you come?"

"I thought . . . "

"What?"

"I thought you didn't want me."

"What?"

"I thought . . . you don't want to be seen with me. That you said things about me."

"That's not true. I never said anything! The guys can be so annoying. I think Dan is hearing all kinds of bullshit from Allie."

He took her hand. His fingers were soft and warm, and sent tingles radiating up her arm.

"I want to see you. I've just been waiting for the right time. You know, when all the guys aren't around. I've worked out the chords to a bunch of new songs, and I want to sing them with you. Come back up to Blackberry Hill. Will you? Okay?"

Reena nodded.

"I have to get back, before they notice I'm gone. Don't be a stranger."

He leaned over and kissed her, quickly and shyly. Then he squeezed her hand, and left. Reena went back inside, and found Sharon lying on her bed.

"Did you find anything?" she asked Sharon.

"Nothing. Why was Ethan here?"

Reena blushed, stifling a giggle as she climbed up on Sharon's bed.

"Oh my god," Sharon said, smiling. "I was totally right."

"Shhh, I hear them." The footsteps were like a storm on the porch, as the raiders were marched back by two counselors from an older division who were on *shmira*.

"Nice try, girls," one of the counselors said, chuckling. "Next time maybe avoid the flood lights over the baseball field."

Allie imitated the counselor's voice, in a sing-song, teasing voice: "Nice try, girls!" Peals of laughter rang out through the dark cabin.

Now the counselor was angry. "I don't want to hear a peep out of this cabin the rest of the night, otherwise you'll all be in Warren's office first thing tomorrow. That means *you*, Berger. In bed! NOW.

We'll be on the porch in case you need a reminder."

Everyone was quiet then, getting into their beds, when Allie's voice piped up again, this time in a loud whisper: "Damn you, Lila. If you hadn't tripped we'd have been home free. Thanks a lot."

"Michael stepped on my flip flop!" Lila said.

"Why don't you just stay back next time if you're going to ruin everything?" Allie went on.

"Allie, I swear!"

"Quiet!" came the counselors from the porch.

"Whatever, you did it. You may as well fess up."

"It wasn't my fault!" Lila murmured, her voice breaking.

"Leave her alone," Reena said.

"What was that?" Allie said. "Did I hear something?"

"Just leave her alone. Leave us *all* alone!"

For once, Allie was quiet.

"So what are we going to do about your things?" Sharon whispered.

"Forget it," Reena whispered. "I don't care anymore."

"What?"

Watching Lila fighting off Allie at every turn had made Reena think of something the angel had said to her on the road; he'd said she must lose her way to find another path. Camp was a place without signposts, where she'd had to find her way at every step. Lila's predicament was exhibit A of the path best avoided. She may have been lost before, but now it was clear what she needed to do.

"Allie can't get to me if I won't let her," Reena said. "If I don't care, then none of them can touch me. And I don't care."

"Well played, Reena Halpern," Sharon said. "Well played."

28

Naomi

The music festival took place the next evening, on the basketball courts. Jim helped Naomi string the mural up over the bleachers. Then they climbed down to look at it from center court.

"Do you think it's straight?" Naomi asked.

"It's . . . I'm speechless, I swear," he said. "It's great. It didn't look the same on the floor. You are exploding with talent, I hope you know that."

Naomi smiled and spun around in place, hardly able to believe it herself. She was pleased with how it had come out. Then she realized that Mara was standing behind them, watching.

"The campers will be here in five minutes," Mara said, looking at a clipboard, avoiding eye contact.

Jim nodded and went to take his place with the band beside the drummer and bassist.

Naomi sat down on the bleachers. She thought Mara might at least say something to her about the mural, but she didn't. Instead, she walked to the edge of the court to greet the arriving campers. She hadn't said a word to Naomi since the night before, when they'd stood together on the hill at Pike's Peak. They'd returned to camp in separate cars. Naomi knew her sister was furious at her. She wondered when they'd have it out.

The festival was over in a blink. Each division stood up in turn and belted out a different Hebrew song, while Jim did his best to get them to sing in unison and in tune. He seemed happy in the role—proudly clapping as each group finished. Then it was all over and the crowds streamed off the bleachers and back to their cabins. She hung around while Jim cleaned up and put away the instruments.

"What about the mural?" she asked.

"Grab scissors and let's cut it down. We don't want to leave it out in case it rains."

She ran to the art room and came back with a pair of scissors. Carefully, they cut the twine that was holding up the mural at the corners. Then they rolled it up and she brought it back to the art room. She realized she'd forgotten the scissors and went back to get them.

When she returned, Jim's guitar case was sitting by itself in the middle of the basketball court, but he'd disappeared. "Jim? Where are you?" she called.

No answer. Naomi listened to the quiet of the night, the sounds of the insects and the frogs and the wind, in the place where an hour before there had been so many voices, so much frenetic noise. Listening, she heard humming, in between the trees. The angel. She looked in his direction, and saw him, humming and dancing to his own music. But she didn't go to him this time. She didn't want to.

"Jim!" she called again.

"Over here."

"Where?"

"Here!" Following his voice, she found him at the side of the bleachers, scissors in one hand. With the other hand, he brushed wood dust off the side of the bleachers.

Naomi saw what he'd just carved, and smiled. "You little vandal."

"No," he said. "I'm an artist. Like you."

Later that evening, after the campers were in bed, Jay came to get Naomi from her cabin.

"Rabbi Shapiro wants to see you in his office," Jay said.

"Now?"

"Yes, now. C'mon."

When she arrived at the office, she found Jennifer

crying, and Greg and Jim pacing angrily. "What's going on?" she said, but they all just shrugged. Jay ushered her inside, and sat beside her as Rabbi Shapiro, the camp director, made it all clear.

"Naomi, do you know why you're here?"

"No."

"We have witnesses who say you were among a group of staff members using illegal substances last night," he said, shaking his balding head side to side. "Using drugs is in violation of your contract as a staff member of Camp Tova, whether you are on camp grounds or off. As such, your employment for this summer is terminated. Your parents have been notified, and you will be expected to leave in the morning."

Naomi stared in silent disbelief. She didn't know if she should defend herself, or deny the charges.

"After all of your years here, Naomi, I have to say, I am extremely disappointed. Please return to your cabin immediately to pack your things. You'll be leaving after breakfast."

Naomi stumbled out of the office into the dark path, where Jim was waiting for her. Jay followed.

"So that's it? We don't get to say a word in our defense?" she said to Jay. "What the hell?"

"He could have called the police," Jay said. "But he didn't. I'm sorry, Naomi. We'll miss you." He looked back and forth between Jim and Naomi. "You guys can have a minute, but then you better get back and pack." He walked away down the path.

"Oh, I get it, so we're being let off easy. But, but . . ." Naomi looked into Jim's brown eyes. But *they* were just beginning. "Someone told on us. Who would do that?"

Jim leaned in. "Mara."

Naomi went red with anger. "How do you know?"

"She was coming out of the office when I first got here. And," he whispered in her ear, "Last night, when you were missing, Greg and I rolled one, and I offered her a toke. She didn't take it." He shrugged his shoulders. "I didn't know."

Naomi, breathing in and out, put her hand on Jim's heart, to try to slow her own increasing panic. "My parents . . . are going to flip. I can't go back there, I just can't." Mara really knows how to turn the dagger, she thought.

Jim covered Naomi's hand with his own two. "So don't. Come with me. We'll take the cash we already made this summer, go on a road trip. Let's get out of here, Nay. Together."

29

Reena

The final night of camp came as a surprise, as if Reena thought she might have stayed there forever. Those last weeks flew by as she was carried along by the routine of each day, so that she moved easily from wake-up to *t'filot* to breakfast to swimming to art to lunch to sports to free time to dinner to evening activity.

She never did get back her things from Allie or Michael or Lila. But she wasn't afraid of them anymore, either. She didn't envy Lila having to manage Allie's moods day in and out. How freeing to simply not care.

She'd stopped thinking about all that she was missing back home in the city, like her friends and her apartment. She'd even stopped thinking much about her Dad. And so, just like that, she found she'd survived the entire summer.

"I told you about the last night of camp, right?" Sharon asked, her eyes twinkling. They were on their way to the banquet, the final dinner of the summer, and had dressed up for the occasion—Reena was wearing a mini skirt and a lavender t-shirt with no stains or holes, and Sharon was in a green dress with a belt. The atmosphere was excited, electric, as everyone walked to the dining hall.

Sharon nudged Reena. "No lights out, no *shmira*. No sleep, of course. Ari asked me to hang out after the banquet." She looked at Reena. "But I want to spend time with you, too."

Sharon's crush on Ari, a quiet but funny boy with whom she had sung a duet in the camp play, was an open secret. Reena could see how excited she was.

"Of course you should go be with him. Don't worry, Sharon. We'll see each other soon in the city, promise. We're only ninety blocks and one subway transfer from each other, right?"

"Right."

—

When the banquet was over, Ethan led Reena out of the dining hall and down the steps to the lake. It was dark and the waterfront was closed, but Ethan hopped over the yellow rope and held her hand as she did the same.

"Where are you taking me?" she asked.

They'd been spending time together, but camp was always so busy and crowded that they were hardly ever truly alone. Sometimes he played guitar and they sang together. Once they took a walk to the lower camp and he introduced Reena to his younger sister. A few times, after the evening activity, they kissed in the shadows between the cabins. She liked kissing him, but she was still getting used to it; it felt strange to be so close to another person that you could taste them, and feel their heartbeat mix with yours. There was only one reason she could think of for him to bring her down to the lake in the dark, and it made her a bit nervous.

The waterfront looked different in the dark. Reena couldn't make out the contours of the sand and felt off-balance, her sandals sinking in unexpectedly. The place where the beach met the water looked like a cliff's edge. The lake was like a mirror during the day, reflecting the clouds and sky and trees. But on this moonless night it was flat and black.

"Come in here," he said, opening the door to the lifeguards' shack.

Reena stayed outside while he disappeared into the small wooden hut. "But we're not allowed."

"Yeah, I know, I just want to show you something." She went in. He shined his flashlight on a large water jug with paper cups on top of it, and a wooden bookcase divided into cubbies and full of sunscreen, towels, bathing suits, and first-aid boxes.

She felt like they were trespassing—this space belonged to the swim staff. "Have you been in here before?" she asked.

"Last week, I cut my toe on a rock when I was pulling in a sailboat. Dave brought me in to give me a band-aid. And I saw this." He shined the flashlight on the side of the wooden bookcase, which was covered with etched graffiti. "What did you say your parents' names were?"

"Naomi and Jim," she said, running her hand over the message, identical to the one that they'd found on the basketball bleachers: "Jim+Naomi."

"My mother must've done it. She was the one who was a lifeguard." In one of Mara's photos, her mother was wearing a bathing suit, and she tried to picture her in the shack, naughtily carving into the bookcase. She must have been happy.

"But look, there's more," he said, pointing the flashlight down to the floor, and reading out loud: "In Memory of Naomi G.H.."

Reena sank down to the floor and ran her fingers over the words. "Why didn't anyone tell me this was here?"

"Maybe none of the lifeguards know that she was your mom."

Reena nodded. She couldn't believe that this had been here all along—even if no one ever noticed it, it meant that here, in this place, her mother's memory was still alive.

"You told me once that your favorite place in camp is the lake," Ethan said. "I bet it was hers, too."

Reena stood up and walked out of the shack, pulling her sandals off one at a time. She liked the way the cool sand felt between her toes. She walked down the beach until her feet were in the water. Her mother had probably stood right here, looking out at the lake.

Ethan came up beside her and took her hand. She squeezed it.

"Let's go in," she said.

"Now?" Ethan asked. "Okay."

Before she had time to think twice, he took her hand and pulled her into the water, clothes and all. She yelped in surprise at the cold water and the weight of her wet shirt and skirt.

"Shhhh!" Ethan said, laughing. She clapped her hand over her mouth.

They swam under the metal dock into the deeper water, into the middle of the empty swim area. When they reached the deep raft, they climbed out and sat side by side. Reena shivered in her wet clothes, and she thought about taking them off, but doubted that it would make her warmer. And it would definitely make her shyer. Ethan put his arm around her. When they kissed, his lips were cold, but his mouth was warm.

"I can't stay out here much longer," she said.

"Can you wait a minute?" Ethan said, taking a pocketknife out of his shorts pocket. "I'm lucky this didn't float away." He started carving into the plank beside him. After working for a minute, he looked up and smiled, "Following in your mom's footsteps, right?"

In the darkness, she could barely make out what he'd written: E + R.

"When you come back next summer you'll get to see it in the light," he said.

———

The last day of camp was short; the buses and parents arrived after breakfast. Over Frosted Flakes and Cheerios in the dining hall, they said their goodbyes. Sharon gave Reena a hug and said, "call me when you get home." She promised she would. They didn't cry like many of the other girls. The histrionics—tears, snot, and hugs—were a tradition, apparently, and Lila was deep in the act. No need for Reena to say goodbye to her; they were going home together.

Reena felt slightly amazed that she knew every face now, when so recently the crowd in the dining room had been a sea of intimidating strangers. The place itself was also familiar now, from the arrangement of the tables and benches, to the giant windows overlooking the lake, to the murals above them.

Her gaze stopped on one mural in particular, and she rose from the table to go stand beneath it. The painting was of a circle of trees, with thick greenery on the sides. In the center was a barefoot man with a beard, smiling and dancing with a girl. *It's me*, she thought. She climbed up on a bench to get closer. In cracking black paint, the artist's signature was clearly visible in the corner: "N. Gordon."

"Here you are," Ethan said, taking her hand and helping her down. "What in the world are you doing?"

"The mural . . . my mother made it."

"Really?" He looked up. "Wow, she left her mark all over this place."

"I know. I can't believe it."

He squeezed her hand as she looked up one more time at the mural. Then they walked together back to the breakfast table to say goodbye to the rest of their friends.

———

As Aunt Mara's car was rolling through the camp gates, Reena stared out the window at Blackberry Hill, its treetops the highest point in the landscape. The week before, she, Ethan, and Sharon went up there and ate the sweetest tiny blackberries Reena had ever tasted.

"But these weren't here a few days ago!" Reena had said, picking and eating them greedily. They were so perfect—wild and fragile.

"They only come out at the end of the summer," Sharon said.

"And they're gone within days," Ethan added.

"So you have to be in the know," Reena said, "and now I am."

She filled her shirt with blackberries and sat in the clearing, looking up at the sky and the passing clouds. The trees swayed in the wind above their heads. *Are you here?* she wondered, thinking of the angel, and then her mother. She ate a blackberry, savoring the sweet juice on her tongue. Had she stayed in New York City that summer, she would never have tasted them. She imagined the angel feasting on the berries day and night. She laughed to herself. Angels don't eat, do they?

Now, on her way out of camp, Reena thought of those blackberries as his gift. He must have shared them with her mother, too. Reena woke up to the sight of striped wallpaper, in two-toned beige, in Uncle Gary's study. The clock on the wall said it was almost noon. She rolled out of the aero-bed, and pulled her hair into a rubber band. She couldn't believe she'd slept so late. She had to get ready; her father was probably already on his way.

In the kitchen, Mara was tossing a salad.

"Rise and shine. You've slept clear through breakfast," she said. "Do you want cereal and toast, or do you feel like lunch?"

"Breakfast I think." She was starving and thought she might be able to manage both meals back to back. "Do you know when my father will be here?"

"His flight is meant to arrive this morning, but no word yet."

"I am going home today, right?"

"Not until we hear from your father. I'm not sending you home to an empty apartment."

Reena exhaled slowly through her teeth. Lila appeared in the doorway, a sour expression on her face. She turned on her heels and headed for the den. Reena heard her click on the TV. Yesterday, in the car, Lila hadn't said a word. She'd fallen asleep as soon as they'd pulled out of camp, and went straight to her room when they'd arrived in Fallwood. Reena couldn't tell if Lila was angry at everyone, or if she was just avoiding her.

Reena didn't think she'd make it another hour in Fallwood. What was she to do? Tip-toe around Lila, and hide in her uncle's study?

Mara came around the marble-topped island and put her hand on Reena's shoulder. "I know you must want to get home, but you're welcome to stay here, anytime, as long as you need. Your father will have had a very long trip."

Reena fought the urge to shake her aunt's hand off her shoulder. She didn't believe her motherliness.

"What's happened with you two this summer?" Mara whispered.

"What do you mean?" Surely, if Mara wanted an explanation, she should begin by asking her own daughter. Reena didn't want to talk to her.

"Ever since we left camp yesterday morning, you and Lila have barely looked at each other, let alone spoken. Something must have happened."

"I don't know," Reena said, taking a piece of bread. "Maybe you should ask Lila."

Mara walked to the door of the den. "Lila, please come in here, dear. I need to talk to you."

"Why?" Lila said.

"Because we need to have a chat."

"Later."

"Now."

Reena took the bread, untoasted and plain, and turned to return to the study, but Mara stopped her.

"Stay," she said. "This concerns you both."

Reena turned around and stood beside the kitchen

counter. Lila shuffled in. Her skin was tanned from the summer sun, and her hair hung wild and loose over her shoulders. They were dressed almost the same—both still in their camp logo t-shirts and cotton shorts.

"How was your summer, Lila?" Mara said.

"Good," Lila answered, picking lettuce leaves out of the salad.

"And you, Reena?"

"Good," Reena said.

"Good," Mara said. "So what's the problem with you two? You both had a good summer, which to tell you the truth I'm quite relieved to hear, because honestly I wasn't sure Reena would be happy at camp." Reena held her breath, waiting for her aunt's point.

"I hoped you would, but I wasn't sure. Lila must have told you that she had a bit of a rough time at first."

Lila pouted, staring at the salad on the counter.

"No," Reena said. "She didn't."

"Well, we all know how it can be, girls and their tiffs. Lila had to find her place, and she did. I'm glad you did, too, Reena. It must be to Lila's credit that you were made to feel so welcome."

Reena turned away. She couldn't do this. There was no way she could explain to her aunt the way Lila had been, the things she had said. Not right now, in their kitchen, with Lila sulking.

"Look," Mara continued, "I may never know what happened between you. But I find it terribly upsetting to see you two not even speaking to each other. I thought this summer would be a great opportunity for you to . . . to . . . rediscover each other."

"Rediscover?" Reena said. "She wouldn't even talk to me. And her friends are witches."

"That's not true!" Lila spat out, her face turning red.

"It wasn't always easy for Naomi and me to get along. But we were sisters, and we did our best to love each other"—Mara's face crumpled, and a tear fell down her cheek. "And then she was gone—"

Lila hugged her mother. Reena had never seen anyone but her dad mourn her mother. The rest of the family always had tried to put on happy faces around her—as if it would be too much for her to be reminded of the unforgettable.

"But she left us something." Mara continued, moving towards Reena and putting her palm on her cheek. "You. You needed me and I took care of you. Once, it was almost like you were mine."

30

Mara

(Thirteen years earlier)

Mara arrived, breathless, at the third floor of her sister's tenement building in the East Village. She'd taken the stairs with her seven-month-old strapped to her in a baby carrier. Standing on the landing outside the apartment catching her breath, she could hear her niece crying. She knocked.

Jim opened the door, his red-faced baby in his arms.

"Mara," he said, backing up to let her in.

Mara had wanted to come earlier, but she was afraid to step on Jim's toes, and also, she'd been comforting her grieving parents. They were all in terrible shock. When Jim called and asked for her help, she knew he must really need her.

Jim looked at his daughter, and when the baby's eyes met his she started to wail again—a desperate, plaintive wail.

"She's not eating and she's not sleeping. What am I supposed to do?" His voice was hard and clipped.

"Let me hold her," Mara said. She released her own baby, placing her gently on the rug in the center of the floor, which was strewn with toys. Then she took Reena from Jim. He sat down on a hard-backed wooden dining chair and watched. Mara swaddled Reena in her arms, whispering a tune in her ear. It was an old Hassidic melody that Naomi had often sung. The baby settled a bit, seeming to recognize the tune, but soon she resumed screaming.

Jim stood up and started pacing. "I don't know what to do with her. She won't take a bottle, and she won't let a spoon near her lips. Hell, I tried giving her ice cream and she wouldn't even take that. I told Naomi she should give the kid real food, but Naomi just nursed her, all the time. Now what do I do?"

"You must be exhausted. Go lie down, I'll take care of her for a while."

"Damn right I'm exhausted."

Mara looked him in the eye. She didn't blame him for being on the edge, but still it made her worry. "I'm here now. Go rest."

"But what about Lila?" Jim said, pointing to the baby on the floor.

"She'll be fine. Go."

Jim pushed a chair out of his way and closed himself into the bedroom.

Mara cradled Reena in her arms and resumed her song. Reena quieted again, and then, looking puzzled and excited, pulled at her aunt's shirt.

What Mara did next was not something she had planned. It was instinctive; a decision made in the automatic part of her brain; the part that, a week earlier, had led her to unflinchingly grab a spider out of Lila's crib. She sat down on the sofa and unbuttoned her shirt from the top, exposing one heavy breast. With a whimper, Reena dove down onto her aunt's brown areola like a swimmer taking a breath.

The apartment was suddenly, blissfully, silent, but for the sound of the baby suckling. "It's okay," Mara said to the baby, but also to herself.

Lila inch-wormed her way over to her mother's feet and whimpered, demanding attention. Mara reached her free arm under the baby's armpit and lifted her to her lap. Then she pulled down the fabric that covered her other breast and gave her what was rightfully hers. The babies' feet became entangled as their hands grabbed onto Mara's shirt, tiny fist by tiny fist. Mara's face was red and streaming with tears as she held on tightly to their heavy bodies as best she could.

—

That same day, Mara took her brother-in-law and niece home with her to New Jersey.

"I couldn't leave them there alone," she told her husband Gary. "Jim can't handle a baby by himself, and in his state."

After the funeral, Jim returned to work, leaving the house early each morning for his commute into midtown. Mara lost herself in the extra effort of caring for two babies, tidying the house, and preparing meals for the men to have on their return from work.

"Talk to him, please," Mara said to her husband one evening as she was washing the dinner dishes. Gary was reading the paper at the round kitchen table. "He just lost his wife. He needs to have a man to talk to."

Later, while the two men were drinking scotch in front of a football game, she heard Gary say to Jim, "What a great girl Naomi was. It's such a tragedy she's gone." And "That poor kid of yours. You two are welcome under our roof as long as you need."

Gary worked long hours as an accountant, and Mara thought that he didn't pay much attention to the goings on under his roof. He didn't notice, for instance, that Mara had got both babies on the same schedule, nursing them side-by-side before each nap and at bedtime. He knew nothing, it seemed, about the unusual bond between her and her niece. Nor did he notice how quiet Mara had become, how little she spoke at dinner.

She and Gary had none of the easy conversations that they used to have. There was too much, now, that she felt she couldn't say. She couldn't explain the weight she felt to make things right, to bridge the canyon between herself and Naomi that had begun that summer when her sister had run off with Jim.

Jim made her uncomfortable, eating silently at their table and never discussing his plans or how long he would stay. Just like in the days when he and Naomi first met, it was almost like he couldn't see Mara at all.

"Mara's just so happy to have you two here," she heard Gary tell Jim. "It's healing for her, taking care of Reena."

It made Mara fume, to hear him say that. As if taking care of Reena was something she was doing for herself. She worried a great deal about her niece. Jim could never be the nurturer that Naomi had been, and that she herself was. It was too late, now, for her and Naomi; she'd never have a chance to make things right with her sister. But it was not too late to do right by her niece.

Mara imagined raising the two girls together into adulthood, like sisters. She was amazed how quickly they had become accustomed to each other. They sometimes woke each other up from their naps in their adjacent cribs so as not to be alone. They crawled around the house following one another, watching one another. Sometimes they cried in argument over a single rattle or doll. On sunny days, Mara put a playpen in the yard and left them to their own devices. They chewed on leaves that fell down from a large maple tree. Or they lay on their backs and held onto their feet, staring up at the flat blue sky through the branches, or listening to the passing birds.

After three months without her, Mara wondered if Reena still remembered her mother. Sometimes, when both babies were hungry, they pushed to get closer to her and cried out to be picked up first. She wondered if Reena had any sense that there was someone else she used to want more. Mara could clearly imagine her sister's mess of curly hair tied behind her head, the single blue ceramic bead tied on a leather string around her neck, the knee-length cotton tunic that she wore throughout the year, alone in summer and over jeans in winter. It was as if Naomi might walk in the room at any minute. But she sensed that for her niece, time was passing quicker; babies can heal overnight. But whether or not Reena was aware of it, the loss would be forever. She wondered if she could ever fill the hole of Reena's loss, and whether Reena could ever fill the hole of hers.

—

Reena's first birthday fell on a Sunday. Mara made a cake, and asked Gary to fetch his camera to record the occasion. He snapped shots of Mara holding a forkful of cake in front of Reena's round face, and of the two babies sitting on a rug with a handful of wrapped gifts between them. Lila ripped into one, but Reena sat with a look of doubt on her face, as if she might cry. Mara sat on the floor and showed her how to stack the wooden rings on the toy that she'd bought. Then Jim picked Reena up and sat her on his lap to show her the present he'd bought—a stuffed bunny—but she wasn't interested in it.

"Mama!" Reena said, reaching for Mara.

Jim put Reena back on the floor and left the room. Mara didn't try explaining to him that that's how Reena said "more" and "my" and "milk" and "Mara." She knew what he had heard, and that was all that mattered.

—

That same night, Lila was already asleep in her crib and Mara was nursing Reena in the rocking chair, when she was startled by the sound of heavy footsteps coming up the stairs. Jim appeared at the door of the nursery and froze, tilting his head to the side, as if that would help him understand. And in that moment Mara felt her head clear and her senses return, the way you can instantly hear better when your ears pop an hour after you've come down off a mountain. She knew it would be the end.

"Give her to me," he said quietly.

"What do you mean?" Mara said. "She's almost asleep, I'm about to put her down."

He came closer, his almost six-foot frame towering above her in the rocking chair. "Give my daughter to me. Now."

As he took her with shaking hands, Reena started to cry, reaching for Mara. But Jim was resolved. Within an hour he had left the house with Reena tucked under his arm, without so much as a thank you to Mara for all that she had done.

31

Reena

Reena's father called in the afternoon and said there wasn't an available rental car in all of Manhattan. So Reena returned to the city the same way she'd left, on the New Jersey Transit bus. While she was getting ready to go, she saw Lila leaning over her backpack. Reena approached her, and they exchanged quick kisses, which was more than Reena expected. The story that Mara had told them was like a fairy tale. And yet, Reena knew it was true. She and Lila had spent months together as babies, like sisters; Mara had once been like a mother to her.

On finishing her story, Mara had hugged her and said, "I want you back, Reena. I want you and Lila to be like sisters. I don't want Lila to repeat with you the mistakes I made with Naomi, and with your dad. I thought you'd finally get a chance to be close, together at camp. But I should have known it wouldn't be easy. Relationships are harder than that."

Reena knew that last part to be true. She wondered what it all meant to Lila.

On the way to the bus station, Reena sat in the passenger seat of Mara's car and watched the windshield wipers do their dance as the car splashed through wet streets. She stared out the window at the strip malls and chain restaurants, and soon the car pulled into the drugstore parking lot that doubled as a bus stop. Mara left the engine running as she waited with Reena for the bus to come.

"You must be excited about starting high school, " she said. "When is your first day?"

"I'm not sure. I guess there must be some letters

about it waiting for me at home."

Reena wasn't in the mood for small talk. Facing forward, her hands on her knees, she decided it was now or never to ask her what was on her mind. "Did my mother have another boyfriend at camp? Someone other than my dad?"

"What a funny question," Mara said, gripping the wheel with both hands, though they were parked. "Where does that come from?"

"Lila told me—"

Mara shook her head.

"So she didn't hear something from you?" Reena rubbed her damp hands together.

"Naomi had her secrets, and I can't pretend I was her closest confidante, at least at that time in our lives, so I truly can't say for sure. But what difference does it make? She loved your father very much, if that's what's worrying you."

"Maybe you remember a man . . . A guy with a beard, who didn't wear shoes? Who liked to sing? Do you remember someone like that?"

"I don't remember exactly, but if I recall, musicians were your mother's bread and butter back in the day. All those Washington Square Park hipsters she met at college." She let out half a laugh. "You know, your father had a beard for a while."

"I'm not talking about my dad."

"Well, I'm not sure who you're talking about. Don't tell me this came from Lila, too."

"No."

Reena knew that the angel had known her mother. There was the photo, and there was the mural. But that didn't mean Mara knew about him. The more she thought about it, the less likely it seemed that Mara would have known. She herself had told no one. Why would her mother have done any different? Reena exhaled and leaned her head against the seat back. *This is between us*, she thought. *Between me and my mother. The angel is ours.*

"Of course you're curious about your mother. You ask me anything you want. Reena, I'm sorry. I really am. I should have been there for you more, I should have and I wasn't. If I could do it all again—"

"No," Reena said. The bus pulled into the parking lot and she opened the door to get out, but then she turned around, leaned in and gave her aunt a kiss on the cheek. "Everything's fine. Thanks for the ride. Thank you for everything."

—

As the bus crossed over the bridge and wound its way downtown, Reena felt energized. She passed through uptown neighborhoods that weren't hers but could have been, as she saw familiar-looking bagel shops, drug stores, groceries, diners, and dry cleaners.

Through the bus window, she saw a girl, maybe six years old, splashing in puddles in her plastic sandals. *That used to be me*, she thought. *A city kid.* By the time she was five she could easily lead a visitor to the deli on First Avenue where her dad bought his coffee. She knew the way to her doctor's office in the Beth Israel building on 17th Street, and the drug store where they got their prescriptions filled. By the time she was eight, her dad would send her to pick up milk or bread or the paper on her own, a five-dollar bill in her pocket. She knew which deli and which market to buy from, and which ones not to set foot into. She learned to know and love even the small details of these routes, like the corner of 18th Street where, on rainy days, a rushing river forced people to leap like hurdlers. She loved the bench in front of Essa Bagel, where you could sit as long as you liked in the morning sun, munching on a bagel easily large enough for breakfast and lunch, filled with an entire tub's worth of cream cheese. She decided that she'd take her father there in the morning. A warm bagel would be just the thing.

At Port Authority, she was dragging her backpack out of the luggage hold beneath the bus when she felt someone standing too close behind her. She spun around, a hand clutching her shoulder bag.

"Reena, my joy," said her father, embracing her. He smelled like old sweaters and soup—the exact smell of their apartment.

She wanted to be cool, to show him that she had survived just fine without him. But she had no reserves of cool left. She cried like a baby in the arms of her dad on the New Jersey Transit platform, the exhaust from the buses blowing in their faces.

—

They went out that night to their favorite neighborhood Chinese place, The Cottage. Reena had been dreaming of chicken lo mein for weeks, and when the food came, she dug in.

"Didn't they feed you at camp?" her father asked, spooning vegetables onto his plate.

"Sort of," she said with a mouthful of noodles.

"You've been awfully quiet all day," he said. "Let's play our story-telling game. You remember it?"

Reena nodded. It had started when she was around five or six. He was frustrated with her because she'd come home from school and he'd ask how her day was, and she'd only say 'good' or 'fine'. So they played a game where she had to tell him three things about her day, and he'd tell her three things about his.

"Yes, I remember. You go first. Tell me something about Japan."

He took a sip of beer and looked up at the ceiling. "Your old dad is a little famous, in Japan."

"What's that supposed to mean?"

"The national paper ran a story about our group, and suddenly our gigs were overflowing. You wouldn't believe the way people love jazz there. I had people in the audience come up to me and they knew everything I'd ever recorded, and where I'd gone to school. It was surreal."

"It must be a let-down to be back in New York after that."

"Not at all. I couldn't wait to get back. I missed you." He ate a bite of rice. "Now your turn."

She pushed her chopsticks around her plate, considering what to tell him first. "I made a new friend," she said, putting a piece of broccoli in her mouth.

"That's nice. More information please?"

"Her name is Sharon and she lives on 110th Street. We're planning to meet up soon."

"Sounds great, assuming she's not a drug dealer."

"Daa-aad. She's not a drug dealer. She's kind of religious, actually. Not that that's a problem. She was really nice to me and not everyone there was." She took a drink of water. "Your turn."

Reena could tell by the worried look in her father's eyes that it was hard for him to hold back from grilling her.

"Let me think," he said. "I got in trouble once for blowing my nose."

Reena raised an eyebrow at him.

"It's true. I had a cold—or maybe it was allergies, I don't know—just the regular post-nasal drip. And one night we were invited out to dinner before a gig with the manager of the club. He brought us to a traditional-style restaurant where you leave your shoes at the door, and sit on the floor."

"You're making me jealous."

"Just wait. You won't be." He smiled. "I ordered soup, and my host encouraged me to put this chili paste in it. Well, having no fear of chili in any form as you well know, I put a spoonful of the stuff in, figuring it would clear out the sinuses to boot. You should have seen his eyes, watching me take the first spoonful."

"Why?"

"Let's just say I exceeded the recommended dose. But I slurped down every strand of udon, and then drank the broth. By the time I was done, my nasal passages were on fire, so I blew my nose in my napkin. I didn't think it was a big deal, but apparently it's very rude to blow your nose in public, and even worse at a meal. My host got up and left the table."

"Dad!" She could imagine this scene. Her father had a loud honking sound to his nose-blowing, as well as a cheerful cluelessness.

"Yes, the waitress came and led me to the bathroom. I got the message, alright."

"That is so embarrassing!"

"I know. They acted like I had just taken a piss under the table."

"Shhh!" she said, putting a finger in front of her mouth, and looking around to see if anyone was listening.

"Okay, that was my story," he said. "Now you again."

She took a deep breath. She may as well tell him all the things that he would find out about soon enough. "I kind of have a boyfriend."

Her father choked on a sip of beer. "I'm not ready for this," he said.

"Not ready for what?"

"Nothing, nothing." He cleared his throat. "Go on."

"His name is Ethan. He's really nice and he plays guitar and he wants to meet you."

"You're not, um . . ." He turned bright red, from his receding hairline to the v-neck of his black t-shirt. "Look, if you ever need to talk to um . . . a woman . . .."

"Thanks, Dad," she said. "But it's not like we're having sex, if that's what you're asking. Geez."

He put his hand on his forehead and exhaled.

"Anyway, he lives upstate; who knows when I'll see him again?" *Hopefully soon*, she thought, filling her mouth with noodles. She missed Ethan, but she didn't want to talk about that. "Your turn," she mumbled.

He sat very still. "I'm sorry, Reena. I said the wrong thing."

She shrugged.

"When you were a toddler," he continued, "and I was having a helluva time taking care of you on my own"—he winked at her, and she smiled—"the head of your daycare told me something that I've never forgotten. She said that just when you feel like you've figured out your kid and gotten things down—whether it's sleeping or feeding or leaving her at school—everything changes. It may have taken me a while, but I figured out how to take care of you. And now you've gone on and grown again, haven't you?"

She didn't answer.

"Of course you have. That's what you're supposed to do. I had a lot of time to think this summer, and I owe you an apology. It was really jerky of me not to give you more of a say about going to camp."

"Yeah," she said.

"But it sounds like maybe it wasn't so bad? Maybe you can forgive me?"

"Forgiven," she said.

He paid and they left the restaurant. It was a cool evening, and Reena pulled a sweatshirt on as they walked along Seventeenth Street.

"You know, I never told you my third thing."

"I'm listening," her father said.

"I know why you've always hated Mara."

"Who told you that I hate her?" He stopped and faced her.

"No one had to tell me. It's not like you ever pretended to be happy to see her."

"I don't hate her," he said, turning and starting to walk away. Reena trotted beside him to keep up.

"Dad, you don't need to pretend. I know what happened. And I don't blame you. That's all I wanted to say."

Her father was silent for a block or two. Then he said, "Mara loves you, and so do I. No one ever said families weren't complicated. You fight, you might not even talk sometimes. But deep down you love them and they love you, no matter what."

"So you love Mara?"

He paused. "I love her for loving you."

———

Reena's camp duffle arrived home on the Friday of Labor Day weekend; she spent the final days of summer going up and down in the elevator to the laundry room in the basement, washing every t-shirt and sock and sheet. She was halfway through the contents of the duffle bag when she found her stationery box under several moldy towels. She sat on the bed and held it in her lap, trying to remember when she had last opened it. She turned it upside-down and watched its contents float down to the blue oval rug: her father's postcards from Tokyo and Kyoto; Grandma's letters, in her swirling handwriting, about playing bridge and buying fish for dinner; a pocket calendar that she got free from Met Foods; two Bic pens; sheets of stationery and matching envelopes.

She started gathering up the mess when she realized she had forgotten to empty her backpack, which was still sitting by the wall. She opened it and right at the very top found a white envelope with no stamp, just her name written in the center in capital letters. She turned it over in her hands several times before opening the flap, which was tucked-in but unsealed. And there was her mother. That is, there was the photo of her mother with Aunt Mara, one of the ones that she'd taken from Lila's house that she thought she'd never see again.

She searched the background for landmarks of the world that she now knew so well. The trees, the water, the sky, all looked familiar, but also different, like the skewed view through a mirror. Her mother's face was a mystery to her, only recognizable from other pictures equally old and faded as this one. But Reena knew Mara now, and she looked happy in the photo, as if she had just heard a joke.

There was another photo in the envelope, too: the one of Mara and her father. They stood close enough to each other to guess that they were friends in their own right. She wondered if that could ever be the case again.

The third picture, the one of her mother with the bearded man she now thought of as her angel, was not there. She closed her eyes, imagining him, his blue eyes and his soothing voice, wishing she could see him again. He knew her mother. There were questions she'd meant to ask him, things she'd never get to say.

But standing in her room just then, she realized she had someone living with her, someone flesh and blood, who could tell her all about her mother. All she had to do was ask.

She opened the white envelope again to double-check that the last photo wasn't stuck inside, and noticed a small piece of heart-shaped pink paper.

On it was written: "I'm SORRY. Love, Lila."

—

Reena and her father took the 6 train to 68th Street and walked west into Central Park.

"Can you believe this sunshine?" her father said. "Very rare for Labor Day. Almost always seems to rain." "It's hot," Reena said. "I need a drink."

"I'll get you a soda. Now where are you two meeting, again?"

"At the Alice in Wonderland statue."

"That's just around the bend, by the lake. You used to play there when you were little."

"I know." She'd wanted to come by herself, but her father had insisted on joining her "for the fresh air."

"I promise to stay out of your way . . . just gonna find a shady spot to read. But do me a favor, don't go off anywhere?"

"Okay, Dad."

He bought her a Coke and then set himself up under a tree a few hundred feet away from the foot of the statue, where Reena sat to wait. Little kids were climbing all over Alice and the Mad Hatter, just like she used to. She felt the sun soaking into her tanned skin. She took a sip of soda, savoring the sweet cold fizz.

Someone sat down beside her, a little too close. She noticed his feet first. Barefoot. Then the black trousers. In this heat? She turned her head and there he was, blond beard, twinkling blue eyes, and a smile to match.

His being there next to her, in a crowd, in the park, took her breath away.

"Welcome," he said. "Praise God for this moment of glory."

Her head was spinning. There was her father reclining on the grass. He had a book in front of his face; he wasn't looking.

"I never saw you again, after that night on the road," Reena said. "Why? What happened?"

"Like all his creatures, I wait for Hashem to show me the way."

She'd forgotten how hard he was to make sense of. She looked around to see if anyone had noticed them talking.

"You told me to follow in my mother's footsteps. I know why, now. You were with her, too. You were showing me the way . . . to find out where I come from, and to heal the rift in my family. And I wanted to say—"

He stood up, so she stopped. Turning towards her, he said, "May the Lord comfort you."

"Thank you," she said. "I wanted to say thank you."

Then he walked away. She watched him dance, in that way of his, through a group of Rollerbladers, and along an uptown path, until he disappeared. She looked again at her father, who was still where she'd last seen him. She was humming the angel's tune when Lila ran over to where she sat. Reena opened her arms and gave her cousin a hug.

About the author

Rachel Mann's stories have been published and performed at Hemingway Shorts, Forward Theater Company, Liars' League NYC, Manhattan Lit Crawl, and the Fish Anthology. Her play, *Class Mother*, was nominated for best play at the Venus/ Adonis Theater Festival. She lives in New York City with her husband and three daughters.

rachelmannwriter.com

Acknowledgments

The first draft of this book was written over cappuccinos and plates of buttery eggs at The Kitchen Table in West Hampstead, London. Since then, many people have lent their thoughts and encouragement. Thank you to: Caroline Goldsmith, for bringing this book to life; Alison Burns, Emily Pedder, and my classmates at City University London; Campaspe Lloyd-Jacob and Justine Solomons, readers and rereaders and friends of the highest order; Elizabeth Edelglass, Ellen Tarlow, Paola De Carolis, Laura Cahill, Caitlin Macy, Paul Blaney, and Elana Matthews, who each lent important insights at just the right moments; Deborah Churchill and Hannah Williamson, adventurer-friends for life; Anna Gusel, who wisely advised me to go to the gym less and write more; Barbara and Charles Mann, who believe in the magic of summer camp; and Josh Rosenblatt, who showed up at camp with skepticism and a guitar, and left with me.